Devlin Taylor is Earth's first ambassador, seeing the universe with his alien boyfriend Zal by his side. But nothing is straightforward when you're the first human on board a spaceship. Devlin and Zal need to keep their relationship hidden for now, and many others on the ship would like to get the chance to explore a new species' anatomy.

New planets, strange worlds, and exciting adventures await Devlin, but when an unknown species tries to board the Chroalian ship, something doesn't add up, and Devlin is left wondering what is going on. Add in homesickness, jealousy, and cultural differences, and Devlin has a lot to learn. Good job Zal is by his side every step of the way.

DIPLOMATIC

LIABILITY

DEVLIN TAYLOR,
EARTH AMBASSADOR , BOOK TWO

REBECCA COHEN

A NineStar Press Publication
www.ninestarpress.com

Diplomatic Liability

First Edition, January 2025

ISBN: 978-1-64890-832-3

Also available in eBook, ISBN: 978-1-64890-831-6

CONTENT WARNING:

This book contains sexually explicit content, which may only be suitable for mature readers, and mentions of drug use.

For T & R

Chapter One

D evlin fastened the buttons of his suit jacket. "How do I look? Suitable for drinks with the captain of a starship?"

"As much as I love you in a suit, and probably even more out of one, I do have to ask if it's really the right attire for your new position." Zal was sitting up in bed, his bright orange hair sticking out at all angles and looking like he'd not long before engaged in several rounds of energetic sex. Which was unsurprising because that was exactly what had happened.

"The Ministry said the office dress code extended to my position as Earth Ambassador, but you might have a point that I should probably consider this the equivalent of your dress uniform."

"I don't have one of those yet. While I wait, the closest thing I have are my ambassadorial robes or my formalwear. And the latter didn't survive the evening after our leaving gala. The ship's quartermaster told me in no uncertain terms that he wasn't a seamstress when I asked him to repair the side seam that somehow got split."

Devlin chuckled at the memory. They had thought it would be their last night together, with Zal leaving Earth at the end of his visit. At that time, Devlin thought he had no way to leave with him. They had been very enthusiastic. "You did get a bit excited, but at least you have a chance of repairing your robe; my poor shirt ended up being put in the rag recycling box."

"I'm sure I can find a way to make it up to you." Zal patted the space next to him on the bed with the point of his tail. "I promise not to damage the one you're wearing."

"Nice try, Zal, but you should be getting ready. You're supposed to be my liaison officer, and I've got a drinks reception in my honour to attend. I don't want to be late."

Zal muttered something Devlin's translator either couldn't or wouldn't translate but got out of bed. "We've plenty of time yet. Let me grab a quick shower. I can hardly turn up reeking of sex with a human."

"For all the crew would know, the smell could be a new cologne you picked up on Earth."

Zal laughed and stole a quick kiss as he headed to the bathroom, naked. "Eau d'Devlin does have a nice ring to it, but the last thing I want is someone else liking your scent. That, and your fuzziness, are all mine."

Devlin loved the pattern of scales that ran over Zal's skin and his tail which now, like often was the case, writhed as if it had a mind of its own. Zal was hairless and, because of it, had a fascination with Devlin's body hair from the first time he'd got his hands on his hairy chest.

Staring around his new cabin, Devlin still couldn't believe he was here. There was no mistaking that the vista outside his porthole was space. He was the first Earth Ambassador and would be travelling on this ship for the equivalent of ten Earth months before reaching Zal's home world, Chroalia. The idea of all the fascinating people he would meet was the icing on the cake of being with Zal. They had thought it impossible, both having given up on finding their happy ever after, yet here they were.

A *ping* came from a panel on the wall by his bed. He wandered over to it. It pinged again, and he saw written in green font: *incoming communication.*

For want of a better option, he tapped the writing and when nothing happened there was a third *ping*. "Hello?" he tried.

The screen came to life and a face appeared. They had bright pink skin and a neatly trimmed purple beard but not a wisp of hair on their head, which made their ears look bigger than they were, especially with their elaborate earrings. "Ambassador Taylor?"

"Yes?"

"I am Dr Golic. You're supposed to report to Medbay once you've settled into your cabin. Where is Lieutenant Catenmir? He was aware of the requirement."

He had a vague recollection that he would have a medical once he came aboard, but Zal hadn't said when. Zal was currently in his shower, removing the evidence of how they'd christened his new bed, and since no one was meant to know they were in a relationship yet, it might give the game away. "Er…"

"According to the location sensors he is in your cabin."

"He's just using the bathroom. Once he's done, I'll have him bring me to Medbay."

"Good." Dr Golic gave him a strange look, which Devlin couldn't decipher. He suspected he was going to get quite a few of those in the first few weeks aboard ship. "Come immediately. That way I can take your base levels before they are contaminated from anything you might imbibe, as I understand you've a welcome reception to attend."

"I'll trot right along."

"Walking will be acceptable, Mr Taylor. There is no need to engage in Earth equine activities."

It took a moment for Devlin to realise what Dr Golic meant. "Of course, no trotting."

"I'll assign you a more suitable exercise plan." He smiled and Devlin thought Dr Golic was trying to be friendly, but he needed more practice. "Inform Lieutenant Catenmir when he surfaces that I have been in contact."

The screen went blank and moments later Zal emerged, a towel wrapped low on his hips, his orange hair slicked back, and the trail of scales as tempting as ever. "Now we're both clean, when do you fancy getting dirty again?"

"Later. Apparently, I'm supposed to be in Medbay now."

Zal stalked forwards. "It can wait."

"Not according to Dr Golic. He called and said you were aware."

Zal scrunched up his nose. "No one said it had to be immediately. I just wanted to keep you to myself for a little while longer. Once we're out there, I'm your liaison, not your lover."

He stepped closer and kissed the tip of Zal's nose. "It won't be for long."

"I suppose it is necessary," Zal said with a resigned huff. "The last thing we want is someone stirring up trouble suggesting you only got the job because you were intimate with me. The Earth Ambassador position is so new, we can't risk someone trying to derail it."

"I know." Devlin understood and agreed completely, but he'd only just got Zal back, and he was going to have to remember to keep his hands to himself when not in either of their cabins.

"We're going to have our whirlwind romance and then the ship will know." Zal grinned. "I'm going to do this properly, Devlin. I suspect your previous boyfriends haven't appreciated how wonderful you are, but I'm not going to make the same mistakes as those stupid humans."

He was right, Devlin's exes hadn't been the greatest examples. He'd been a convenience, an undemanding partner, and his last one had called him dull before he'd dumped him. Hadn't stopped Grant crawling back, but Devlin had been wise to him, and Zal had turned up and whisked him away before he'd told him where to go.

"Should I be worried about what you mean by doing this properly? So far we've had a lot of sex, and I've seen your ability to eat your own body weight in carbs, so if that's what your courtship rituals entail, then we're near enough married."

"Humans might not understand the concepts of romance and courtship, but I assure you, this Chroalian is from the Talpi region, and we're known for being the most wonderful and attentive lovers."

"I've experienced how attentive you are, and I can't wait for you to show me more, but first you'd better get dressed and take me to Medbay. I don't want to get into trouble on my first day. They might send me back."

Zal collected his clothes and dressed. "If anyone will get in trouble, it'll be me. So unless they can somehow find a field-certified xenobiologist with level six clearance, there's no way either of us is in any danger of being thrown off this ship for you being late to Medbay."

"Please, Zal, I need to make a good impression. It's important to me." As much as he'd taken the role of ambassador to be with Zal, he knew he also had a huge responsibility to the people of Earth not to fuck it up. If humans wanted the chance to explore the universe, he needed to show that as a species they could prove themselves worthy to do so.

"I'm sorry, Devlin. You've always been a true professional. One of the many things I love about you is we have a similar work ethic."

"That's another thing. You have your own job aboard ship, and I need to get to know people and have them respect and want to spend time with me. Otherwise I'm going to have a pretty lonely existence."

"I should be able to take a few days off research duties to help you settle, but you're right: you do need to be able to function without me as a constant shadow." He took hold of Devlin's hand. "We'll still be spending a lot of time together, but all couples need a bit of space and outside interests."

"I'm sure you'd be trying to throw me out of an airlock if we were together every waking moment." Although he did agree with Zal, he couldn't say he wanted to hear it in such a blunt way so soon after he'd left his home planet to be with him. "I'm sure I'll find plenty of ways to occupy myself."

Zal frowned. "Don't go reading more into this than what I meant. Of course I'll want to be with you as much as possible. I can see I'm going to have to spend a lot of time reprogramming your conditioning. Your exes seem to have done more damage than I thought."

He'd not had the best of luck with men, but he was hardly a desperate heroine in an old-fashioned romance novel in need of being rescued. To be fair to his exes, he'd not been that devoted either, putting his job first, although it might have been more of a reaction to how they'd treated him to start with.

"Don't be daft. I'm trying to agree with you." He smoothed down a tuft of Zal's hair that stuck out now he was drying. "I suspect it'll be a slow start, but before I know it, I'll be up to all sorts of things."

He'd not exactly been given much time to prepare for his departure, and the Ministry had an overarching idea of what the values and behaviours of an ambassador would have, but they'd not fleshed out his day-to-day duties as there was simply no way of telling what his life on board an alien ship would be like.

"Just be you, and everyone will love you. But not like how I love you because that's not allowed."

Devlin chuckled at Zal's reaction. "I think you might be overplaying my popularity. I'm sure the crew won't be intrigued by a human. I'm just another alien, and I'm sure they've seen plenty of others."

"There's a handful of non-Chroalians on the ship, but the crew has never had the chance to be with a human, and you're here for an extended period. I fear you may have a few trophy hunters after you." He wrinkled his nose. "I know there's a number of ensigns who bet on how many different species they can sleep with in one rotation."

"Well, you know I won't let them add me to their list." He couldn't claim to know all of Zal's nuances and foibles, but he was surprised he seemed this worried. "Even if you don't trust them, you can trust me."

"Oh, of course. Sorry, Devlin. I'm not used to caring so much about someone, and for a couple of weeks, while we need to pretend to get to know each other, the rest of the crew might think they have a shot. I know they haven't, and I will try my best not to act like a gumping tosdil."

Devlin thought that sooner rather than later he might need to start learning Zal's language because no matter how good the translator was there were going to be words it couldn't cope with, although it was pretty obvious what those meant. "Don't worry. I'll tell you if you're being a prat."

The thrill of being aboard an alien spaceship intensified as they left Devlin's cabin and headed into the corridor. "You mentioned there's a handful of non-Chroalians on the ship."

"Yes, it might be nice for you to get their perspectives. You're meeting one now. Dr Golic is a Driolsan."

"I don't know that species."

"They've not been in contact with Earth. Their planet is peaceful, and they generally don't travel outside of their own solar system. Golic's a bit of a rarity, good doctor though."

The corridors were quiet and Devlin was a little disappointed, having envisioned the ship to be a constant hustle and bustle. "Where is everyone?"

"Everyone on the ship has a job to do, and given it's not long until the end of shift, they're probably at work or about to start. Don't worry. You'll see lots of people soon."

They took an elevator down several levels to one which was

labelled C deck and Devlin realised that it probably wasn't a C in the human sense as it was in between decks with Chroalian non-Latin-looking letters. Which meant there wasn't really an H deck either and he'd need to stop thinking in human terms.

The doors opened into a lobby. A beam of light scanned him as he walked forwards.

"Taylor, Devlin. Human. Unknown condition. Dr Golic is waiting for you in station seven for your appointment."

"What was that?" Devlin asked, looking around to see where the voice had come from.

"Virtual receptionist. Acts as a triage and, if you don't have an appointment, it'll get you booked in; don't expect it to be overly helpful though. It's as if it's had that part of its sub-routine redirected, and no one can figure out how to change it."

"Good to see there are some universal truths," muttered Devlin, remembering the stern young woman at his old doctor's, who seemed to thrive on keeping as many patients away as possible.

A door opened and Devlin took that to be station seven. Dr Golic appeared. "Ah, at last. You needn't stay, Lieutenant."

"As Ambassador Taylor's liaison I have been assigned to help him settle into life on this ship. This will be a new situation for him so I am here to support him. If *he* wishes me to leave, I will do so at *his* request," Zal said, and Devlin could see him bristling at the attempt to send him away.

It might look a bit odd to have Zal remain, especially for

something private like a medical, but Devlin didn't want him to go. "I'd rather he stay"

Dr Golic sighed. "Very well, but I have questions to ask that are usually confidential. So if at any time you want him to leave, I will eject him for you."

Zal's eyes narrowed so he suspected Zal didn't want to be sent away but couldn't argue without revealing more about their relationship than they wanted at this time.

Dr Golic was ushering them in. "The transporter took some readings when you beamed aboard, and I've received your medical records from the preliminary screens conducted by your Earth physicians. Very helpfully, they also sent a comprehensive database relating to your species' health requirements and potential maladies. According to those, you're in good health," Golic said, but in such a way that suggested he didn't trust what he'd read. "But I would not be performing my duty if I didn't run a more comprehensive check and confirm a few results."

"Okay." He'd been lucky health-wise so far and hadn't needed to see many doctors, and the few times he'd seen his GP, he'd been in and out in minutes. He didn't think that would be the case with Dr Golic, and he suspected the prospect of attending a human had piqued his curiosity. "Do you want me to undress?"

"Oh no, just lie down." He patted the padded bench in front of him. "I appreciate you're from a much more primitive species, medically speaking, but you should know, in general, I don't ask people to take their clothes off."

Zal snorted from where he'd taken a seat. Dr Golic ignored him and consulted what looked like a small computer somewhere between a tablet and a games console. "The surface underneath will vibrate for a few seconds, followed by a set of scans. Nothing to worry about."

Devlin did as he was told and found the bench surprisingly comfortable. "I had regular health checks for my previous position—I doubt there's anything to find."

"It's not a matter of finding anything, but making sure I would know if there was a difference if you were to come to me in the future. I've not had the pleasure of dealing with your species, so it's best not to make incorrect assumptions from the beginning." His eyes seemed to shine at the thought of getting his hands on Devlin's medical data. He tapped something into his device. "Right, while the scans run, I will go through a number of questions, some you may have answered recently, others not. Acceptable?"

"Yes." He could hardly refuse, and he was intrigued by how different the medical practices would be from what he was used to.

"You've no known allergies to Earth antigens, have no addiction to Earth tobacco or narcotic substances, and you're not sexually active. Correct?"

"Well, yes to the first two, but the last one isn't technically correct."

"I'm not including masturbation. According to the records

from two weeks ago, you were marked as not having regular inter-course with another person."

"Surely whatever I did on Earth isn't relevant to now."

"Ah, some sort of final fling, I believe the Earth colloquialism is. Something to remind yourself of what you've left behind." Golic seemed proud of getting the lingo right.

Devlin needed to be careful how he answered this, not just because of his and Zal's relationship, but also he didn't want Zal thinking he'd had some sort of fling when he'd in reality been pin-ing away. "Not exactly. But it's a private matter."

"Nothing should be private from your doctor. I'll run a wider screen for sexually transmittable diseases and anything specifi-cally carried in semen and vaginal fluid."

"I'm sure your files make it clear I'm homosexual."

Dr Golic raised an eyebrow and re-read his notes. "Ah, apol-ogies, I misread. For some reason I thought you were hermaphro-ditic but male projecting, like myself and my own species." He tapped his device a few times and peered at the screen. "But now I see you most definitely don't have a vagina. I can take you off the regular cervical screening list."

"You'd have trouble screening something that isn't there."

"Quite. Now back to your sexual activity. When did you last have penetrative sex?" Dr Golic glanced in Zal's direction. "Per-haps Lieutenant Catenmir should step outside for a few minutes. Your sexual activity is none of his concern."

Something beeped and Dr Golic stared at the results, his eyes widened. "Or maybe it is."

"Er…?" Devlin looked over to Zal who was sitting with his arms crossed over his chest.

"It seems that you have traces of Chroalian DNA on and in your person, and multiple contusions across your chest." He cleared his throat. "You've only just come on board but there's nothing in your notes about your tendency to indulge in intercourse so readily or that you are promiscuous by nature."

"What are you insinuating?" Devlin asked, confused.

"Hmm, but there are traces of titular wine in your bloodstream." Dr Golic rounded on Zal. "Did you give him titular wine with the purpose of pursuing sexual gratification?"

Zal got to his feet. "I do not like your tone. I think there has been some misunderstanding."

Devlin's brain was finally catching up. Golic either thought he'd had sex with Zal because he has a sexual drive too great to contain his desires, and the last thing he needed was to be earmarked as an easy lay. Or that Zal had used the wine to make him malleable. Neither was true, and neither would help them in the future.

"Are you bound by patient confidentiality?" Zal asked.

"Of course I am. Why would you ask such a question?"

Devlin guessed where Zal was going with this, but he'd let him take the lead on how to handle the doctor.

"I think that's obvious, Dr Golic. The reason Devlin has Chroalian DNA about his person is it's mine. And there was absolutely no coercion involved on either side."

"Lieutenant, I am not judging either of you for engaging in sexual gratification; it is perfectly natural to be interested in what it would be like to have sex with someone from a different species. I will just adjust the files to highlight that Ambassador Taylor should be tested at an increased frequency due to his elevated need for intercourse." Dr Golic gave Devlin what he thought was an attempt at a smile. "If you are non-monogamous by nature, I will need to know if I should be introducing a general screen for Earth diseases for the crew. As far as I know, most are non-communicable to Chroalians or the other species on board, and the standard wide-spread vaccines should cover them, but it's better safe than sorry. As the ambassador for Earth, I suppose it is one way to 'win friends and influence people'."

Devlin almost choked on his tongue. The doctor thought he was going to fuck his way through the crew. He didn't know how things had spiralled away from him so quickly.

"Absolutely not," snapped Zal. "If you'd given me a chance to finish you'd have heard me say that what occurred between us was not an isolated event. I have been intimately involved with Devlin Taylor since my time visiting Earth. In fact, part of the reason he agreed to become Earth's first ambassador was due to our relationship—a committed monogamous one."

Dr Golic's eyes widened. "Ah, well, that is different. But why aren't you listed as his partner?"

Zal took a step over to Devlin and then took his hand.

"Because, apart from my parents, you're the only one who knows. We didn't want to call into question Devlin's credentials for the position in case someone tries to make trouble."

"I see. Medical records are confidential and encrypted, and it would be better if I could list someone as Ambassador Taylor's emergency contact."

"That would be me." Zal smiled. "I would also appreciate it if you could similarly update mine to include Devlin in addition to my parents."

"Consider it done." Dr Golic smirked. "At least, since neither of you is capable of carrying a foetus, I don't need to worry about an unwanted pregnancy. If you were to embark on parenthood, I would highly recommend waiting until after you've finished travelling; research ships are no place to bring up a child."

"I think it will be a while before we start having those sorts of conversations," Devlin said as Zal made his own spluttering noises.

The bench he was lying on stopped vibrating, and Dr Golic consulted his device again. "I don't see anything for immediate concern. I'd like to take some blood. I'll give you something to collect urine and ejaculate samples."

Devlin sat up. "Why would you need a sperm sample? We've already told you the nature of our relationship."

"It's nothing to get excited about. I take samples of all suitably equipped crew members. I didn't see the tests listed in the human databases, so while your outdated screening procedures don't routinely sample sperm, I do. Changes to sperm can be very eluci-dating and spot early onset of numerous medical conditions."

Devlin decided not to argue and instead held out his hand as instructed and Dr Golic placed something that looked like a piece of sticky tape over a vein on the back of his hand. Moments later, without even a prick of pain, the bubble filled with his blood. "Wow!"

Dr Golic chuckled. "None of those nasty needles here. All done. If I get anything back from the tests, I'll be in touch. Other-wise, you'll receive a check-up monthly, and we will remotely monitor your physiology to make sure space travel doesn't inter-fere in any way."

It made sense, but Devlin would have preferred to have been informed directly. Then he realised that this wouldn't be only for his best interests. "Will you be providing me with a report for Earth? I expect my management might like to receive some feed-back on how I was adapting to being off-world."

"Yes, but I will pre-agree any content with you, as it's your data; although it could be useful to extrapolate information for po-tential future ambassadors."

"Appreciate it."

"I'll see you at your reception in a little while," Dr Golic said. "I believe Captain Holjin is keen to make you feel as welcome as possible."

He saw Zal roll his eyes but didn't say anything until they were back in the elevator alone. "I sense you don't like Captain

Holjin much."

Zal huffed. "He's all right and a decent captain, I suppose. But as the captain he tends to think he can have whatever, or who-ever, he wants. Everybody thinks he's great, even my mum."

"Is there some history here I should know about?" Devlin asked. "Otherwise, you do seem a little reactionary, and I've al-ready told you I'm not interested in anyone else. I didn't think Chroalians were generally prone to jealousy as a species."

"We're not. I'm not... most of the time."

Zal's cheeks flushed, but he didn't get the chance to continue as the door opened into the communal area where the welcome reception was being held. Something to file away for later. For now, he'd slap on his best smile because this wasn't the place for that type of conversation.

Now was the time for him to show them why he'd been cho-sen to be Earth's first ambassador. There were far more people than he was expecting, and Devlin suspected every one of them would want to talk to him. He thanked his lucky stars it was a good job he was excellent at remembering people's names.

Chapter Two

Zal accepted a glass of low-alcohol wine as they joined the welcome reception. He'd already shared a drink with Devlin earlier in the day, and he knew that if he were to drink too much he'd end up a giggling mess as alcohol and anti-gravity were not a kind combination for his system. He was also acutely aware that Holjin was likely to be in full captain mode, so he wasn't about to leave Devlin's side. He'd experienced what it was like to have Holjin's undivided attention, and while it had been a good fuck and a fun way to try and get over Telgan, he wasn't about to let his boyfriend anywhere near him. As predicted, Holjin was heading in their direction.

"Ambassador Taylor, Devlin," Holjin corrected himself and held up his hand in greeting. "I hope your cabin is comfortable and you've been able to see a bit of my ship."

He was attractive, tall with broad shoulders, and bright-blue spikey hair. His eyes already had a tinge of purple, a sure sign of his desire for Devlin. Zal had to remind himself he wasn't here as Devlin's lover and could not weigh in and defend his territory even though every one of his instincts told him to.

Devlin pressed his hand to Holjin's and Zal had to stamp down on an inexcusable wave of jealousy. He'd never been one to be possessive or jealous but Holjin brought out a side of him he didn't like, and he would need to make sure it didn't manifest elsewhere. He'd even been in a loose triad at one point and had shared with others in the past when not in a committed relationship. If nothing else, he needed not to let it get the better of him or he was going to reveal more than he should.

"Yes, I've had a quick tour, an adventure in the Medbay and have started to unpack my things. Although I am very excited to explore more and meet the crew."

"I'll clear some of my schedule tomorrow, give you a captain's view of the ship, our mission, and my personal perspective."

"I'm sure you're far too busy," Zal said, before Devlin even had the chance to open his mouth. "I've got most of it covered."

"Nonsense, Zal. Devlin is an honoured guest. It would be unforgivably rude if I were not to."

Devlin cleared his throat, and Zal saw he was giving him a look somewhere between confused and exasperated, but he couldn't be completely sure as his expression might mean something different for humans. "That would be very kind of you,

Captain. I can't monopolise Zal's time either, and I would like to get to know others on board."

"I've a little surprise for you." Holjin bounced on the balls of his feet and his tail writhed, which Zal knew meant he was feeling smug.

Holjin waved over an ensign who was carrying a plate with a domed lid. Holjin lifted it with a flourish. "I heard you were a big fan of Earth biscuits, so I've had our chef download several recipes, and he's whipped up a batch of chocolate digestions."

Devlin's face was a picture of happiness and Zal hated Holjin for being so fucking thoughtful.

Devlin picked up a chocolate-covered biscuit in awe. "Thank you so much. They're digestives, and it's very wonderful of him to do so."

"We all want to make you welcome, Devlin. The chef loves trying new recipes, but he did say he's still working to perfect something called a ginger nut," Holjin said, sounding bemused. "But he's happy with these."

Devlin took a bite and grinned. "These are great."

"I've also taken the liberty of having a selection of human delicacies brought aboard, including a large quantity of tea."

Zal seethed. He'd had a similar idea, but the opportunity to surprise Devlin with his small but specially curated stash hadn't yet arisen. Now Holjin was receiving all the grateful smiles and would get the credit whenever Devlin reached for something to remind him of home. How dare Holjin be such a considerate bastard.

Holjin took hold of Devlin's elbow. "Let me begin by introducing you to a few people."

Zal knew this would happen. He wanted to be the one escorting Devlin around, not Holjin, and he would stick close by to ensure a certain captain's hands and tail didn't wander. Holjin and Devlin made for a striking couple but Zal refused to let the idea take root. Him and Devlin were together. No one else might know that yet, but Holjin wouldn't change what they had. That wouldn't stop Zal from getting annoyed at Holjin though.

They were welcomed into a small huddle of three Chroalians who were members of the bridge crew. "My second in command is at the helm this evening, but I'll introduce you to Commander Sihil tomorrow. In the meantime, these fine fellows are my Chief Tactical Officer, Commander Strass," said Holjin, indicating an officer who had Zal's build, but none of his intelligence, and a penchant for braiding his red hair into something akin to a birds nest.

"Commander Brilli, Chief Communications Officer." He smiled warmly, and Zal noticed he'd dyed his hair pink. Zal had had lunch with him a couple of days ago when it was still his natural yellow colour. He would need to ask what was behind it and if his bond-mate, Appla, had approved. Although he should also probably warn Devlin about how close a friendship he'd had with Brilli and Appla at one time before he heard about it second-hand. They were still two of his best friends, so he didn't want Devlin to misconstrue anything. Most humans hadn't grasped the concept of polyamory, and while he had no desire to practise it with Devlin, it wasn't uncommon amongst Chroalians.

"And Dr Lian, Chief Science Officer." In theory, Lian was Zal's boss, but he had been more than happy to let Zal get on with whatever he wanted as long as he didn't blow up a lab or kill anyone. Lian had bigger problems to deal with after one of his team got infected with an alien pollen that caused a nasty rash and highlighted several shortcomings with the ship's containment protocols.

They all greeted Devlin warmly, and the conversation was kept to small talk and promises of introducing Devlin to their teams, not that Zal was listening, since he was more concerned with how Holjin's hand had moved to rest on the small of Devlin's back. Zal smirked as Devlin collected another drink and repositioned himself out of arm's reach without causing a scene. Holjin wrinkled his nose behind his glass and Zal had the feeling Holjin thought the game was afoot, but Devlin was not the sort to be played with.

The arrival of his parents was a welcome distraction. Even Captain Holjin couldn't monopolise Devlin once his mum was on the scene. "Devlin, you look so at home aboard a starship," she said, and Zal was surprised to see her greet him with an Earth-style kiss on either cheek.

"You're looking as radiant as ever, Scrillia."

Zal relaxed; his mum knew of Holjin's reputation and had been most amused that Zal had been one of his notches. Now, she had planted herself right between Holjin and Devlin. "Captain

Holjin, I see you're making sure the new ambassador is being taken care of," she said and raised her eyebrow.

"You know me, Scrillia, I want to make sure everyone on board my ship gets the attention they deserve."

"I do know you, Holjin"—she patted his arm—"and not everyone needs or wants such attention. Remember, Devlin has Zal as his liaison."

Holjin chuckled. "Zal is also well aware of how generous I am with my attention. I'm sure he can advise Devlin that I'm worth spending time with."

The comment caused several sniggers. Zal fumed and he saw Devlin wince. He couldn't even challenge because no one was meant to know about them, and for all Holjin's lascivious ways, he didn't press his suit on someone who had a partner. Then there was the matter that he hadn't told Devlin he'd slept with Holjin, which was much more likely to be an issue to Devlin than Holjin's current actions. Zal had told Devlin he'd slept with someone after he'd split up with Telgan, but for all he knew, Devlin might assume he'd been with Holjin since he'd returned from Earth.

"I'm sure I can make my own decisions," Devlin said, smiling. "But I can't be seen to be playing favourites."

Devlin really was lovely, and Zal noticed several others in the group wearing the same smitten expression. He was suddenly glad he'd taken steps to romance Devlin properly, as he deserved, starting with what he had planned for later once this tedious reception finished. He caught his mum's eye, and she winked at him. Not for the first time he thought she could read his mind.

The faces rotated around them, many keen to be introduced to Devlin, thankfully, the numbers started thinning, and Zal thought that would be a good cue to whisk Devlin away. They'd not eaten anything apart from the biscuits. He hoped Devlin would love what he had planned for after the soiree.

Holjin receiving a call from the bridge was the perfect opening to make their excuses to leave. "Let's go and find some dinner. I thought I'd also show you one of my favourite places on board."

"I am getting a bit peckish. It means I'm hungry. I don't want to peck you."

Zal laughed. "Not the strangest of your Earth sayings, but thank you for pre-empting my question."

They turned to leave and were stopped by his mum. Scrillia put her hand on Zal's arm. "I meant to tell you, Zal, I'd like to have breakfast with Devlin in the morning."

He wondered what she was up to. "Okay, we can be at the mess for 0800."

"Not both of you, I meant just me and Devlin."

He frowned. "Why?"

"Because I want to discuss aspects of the ambassador programme that will bore you stupid. Don't worry, I won't tell him any stories from you growing up, and I'll keep the baby photos for another occasion."

"I'd love to have breakfast with you." Devlin grinned.

"Don't worry, Zal. I know you said you'd put time aside for

me, but you've already been away from your lab a couple of days. I'm sure you'll benefit from the chance to catch up."

Devlin wasn't wrong, and although it wasn't how he'd expected to spend their first full day of Devlin being aboard, it made sense that Devlin needed to start his job as ambassador in earnest. "I suppose so."

"Good. You can come and rescue your mother from my boring anecdotes."

"Come to my cabin in the morning, and we can have breakfast in my consulting room." Scrillia smirked. "From what Zal's told me, there's nothing boring about you."

Chapter Three

Devlin had been to enough welcome drinks to know there was never enough food, the small talk was repetitive and, generally, most people were only there because they'd been told by their management that they had to turn up. Having said that, it would have been far worse if something hadn't been arranged as it would have screamed that the captain was not happy to have him on board. However, he could have done without Captain Hotpants's overt attempt to flirt and take any chance he could to put his hands on him. At one point he thought steam might come out of Zal's ears, his annoyance so evident, but if he understood Holjin's comment correctly, Zal and the captain had history. He had no problem with Zal having a past, but it seemed Zal wasn't happy about something so, at some point, Devlin was going to have to ask. But not tonight. No, tonight was his first night aboard a spaceship, and nothing was going to spoil it.

"I'm sure the mess was back there," he said, looking over his shoulder. His stomach had let him know that it had been far too long since he'd eaten anything substantial and, while the biscuits were lovely, the alcohol wasn't helping matters.

"Oh, I've arranged for something much better than the mess." Zal's smile was playful, and if they'd still been on Earth he'd have kissed him right there. "Let me just double-check on something, and we'll be on our way."

Zal trotted over to a panel, and his fingers flew over its surface. Devlin had no clue what the writing said but, for once, he didn't mind being kept in the dark as he wouldn't spoil his own surprise. He saw Zal's tail flick and he was beginning to recognise the non-verbal signals he didn't think Zal noticed he was giving out. The jiggle and quick rotation of the arrowhead-like tip was a good sign.

"Ready?" he asked as Zal re-joined him.

"Yes."

"And?"

"You'll see."

He followed Zal to the elevator, where he noticed him select the top button. "Come on, tell me what it is you're up to."

Alone in the elevator, Zal took hold of his hand, squeezed it, and then let go. "You're so impatient. Where's the calm and collected Devlin Taylor I fell in love with?"

"Cheeky."

The elevator opened into a long, softly lit area, with several occupied tables and closed doors across the back wall. The light was significantly less harsh here, and there was a slight blue hue. "We're at the top of the ship. This is a relaxation zone called the Bubble Bar, and behind each of the doors is a viewing bubble."

"Oh, that sounds exciting."

"The bubbles are my favourite places on the ship. I come here to think, and I spent a lot of time here after I left Earth. And this particular viewing bubble is the best of the lot. I was so lucky I was able to use your ambassador privileges to book it, as it's usually not available to crew without special permission."

Devlin squeezed his hand. "I can't wait to share it with you."

Zal made a soft squeaking noise, another sign he was excited, then pressed the door release which emitted a low hiss as the door slid open. Zal pulled him inside. Devlin's jaw dropped as he took in his surroundings. They were in a glass dome, a completely clear canopy, giving the impression they were standing amongst the stars. "Wow!"

"I know, isn't it amazing? The other bubbles are great, but they're basically rooms with extra-large portholes. But this is full immersion."

He spun slowly around on the spot, looking up into outer space. It was almost too surreal to comprehend. He'd had lots of thoughts about life on board but never had he imagined this. Then he spotted the table and chairs and what looked like a picnic basket.

"We're eating here," he said, still a little thunderstruck.

"Yes, the purser was surprisingly willing to indulge our special guest. He's had the chef put together a selection of cold food to introduce you to Chroalian cuisine. I did ask for hot options but he made a most rude snorting noise."

"Whatever we eat, it will be incredible in here. Can I take some photos? I'd like to include a couple in my report, but I'd also like some for us, to record this for posterity."

"You and me both."

Devlin whipped out his phone, then pulled Zal into a one-arm embrace and took a picture of them with the universe as the backdrop.

They took their seats at the table, and Zal began searching through the hamper, making happy little noises as he did so. Zal had been led by his stomach when on Earth, and Devlin had thought it was because of the effect Earth had on his metabolism, but Zal seemed to be as keen on eating his fill wherever he was.

"Right, we'll start with these."

Zal placed three boxes on the table and opened their lids. Devlin leant in to see what was on offer. He'd never been a picky eater—it wouldn't have served him well if he had been—since who knew what sort of delicacies he'd have to try for his new job. He was more intrigued than wary at what Zal was now putting on his plate. An orange spiral sat next to a pile of what looked like thick, dark-red leaves, and finally, a mound of tiny white beads that reminded him a bit of caviar.

"These are all savoury appetisers, designed to trigger your taste buds for the main event."

"I seem to remember you complaining about being served canapes on Earth, and these don't look too dissimilar, if I'm honest."

"No, I moaned about only being fed mouth-sized portions of air and froth—these are far more substantial and, as I said, these are a prelude, not the whole meal."

Devlin chuckled at Zal's indignance. "What have we here then?"

Zal pointed to the orange spiral. "That is bleckleberry rice cake. From my limited knowledge of Earth food, it'll be a bit like the sushi we had but less fishy, and goes really well with the red choi salad, which are the leaves next to it."

Due to their size, Devlin wasn't sure whether he should eat them with his fingers, but Zal was picking up a fork so he followed his lead. "And the white balls?"

"Protein pearls. They're like nuts, quite salty. Nothing like those horrible fish eggs you have. Hang on, let me see if there's something to drink; otherwise it might be unpleasant."

Zal pulled out a flask of pinkish liquid. "Oh, this is lovely. Fruit water, really refreshing, but alcohol-free. Because if I were to drink any more there'd be no way I'd be able to celebrate your first night aboard the *Endeavour* as I planned."

"We've already christened my bed—more than once."

"But not mine." Zal reached out and stroked the back of his

hand. "I got new quarters with my grade and position, and there's been a definite Devlin-shaped hole in my personal space."

Earlier, during his call with Dr Golic, he said he knew Zal was in his cabin, if the ship could tell where they were, then surely that could be trouble. "Wouldn't it be a bit suspicious if I was in your room overnight? I can hardly say I stayed over because it was too far to get home or had a nightmare and crawled in with you."

Zal wrinkled his nose. "I suppose you've a point. We will need to sleep apart, just while we're getting to know each other, then it will look like our romance blossomed on board."

"Or we could just say we couldn't contain ourselves and fell into bed together. From the vibes Captain Holjin was giving out, I don't think he was intending to romance anyone, just move straight to sex."

Zal speared his bleckleberry rice cake and waved it at Devlin. "You don't want to cultivate a reputation like Holjin's, or you'll have half the ship wanting to fuck you."

"I'm only interested in one Chroalian doing that."

"I know, but they don't. And Chroalians can be a bit over-friendly at times by human standards, so just be warned that you're going to get quite a lot of attention."

He wondered if he should ask about what happened between Zal and Holjin but didn't want to sour the mood, as Zal didn't seem to be worried about the rest of the ship, but he was giving off jealous vibes over the captain. Maybe in the morning, or after he'd had breakfast with Scrillia. That might be a better idea as he could get some background on Holjin from Zal's mum.

He tried a bit of the choi salad and rice cake together. It was tangy, with a sharp crunch, and then scooped up the protein pearls, which fizzed in his mouth. "I like those. Everything is really different, yet works so well together." He nudged Zal under the table with his foot. "Like us."

Zal smiled beautifully. "I wouldn't say we were that different. Imagine if you were a gas being. That would be inconvenient."

"Or semi-solid. One of my arrivals on Earth once told me about a species they'd met who, when they reproduced, melted into a puddle and then reformed as a mix of each other."

Zal laughed. "That'd be the ultimate damp patch. Could you imagine mopping up afterwards and finding you'd accidentally wiped up a bit that should have been a leg?"

"A leg wouldn't be the worst part to lose." He smirked. "What if you didn't combine equally? You could end up with two cocks and no arse."

"I'm pretty sure this is not the sort of thing an ambassador should be contemplating," Zal teased.

"True, but I don't think the aliens that came to Earth were the strangest out there, or they wouldn't have been able to adapt."

He finished off his appetisers and was delighted to be served a pre-assembled plate of several different foods beautifully arranged in an array of colours. "The closest this translates to is rainbow for the mouth," explained Zal. "It's a mix of different meats and vegetables traditionally served at celebrations. To be honest,

I didn't think the ship's chef would have known how. They tend to be created by specialists for events like naming and bonding ceremonies."

"I'm honoured, then. Especially on top of the biscuits."

Zal pouted. "I wish I'd thought to do that when you came aboard."

"You arranged all this—and you'll be showing me your world. I was always going to be welcomed by you on the ship, but not by others, so Holjin arranging the biscuits was a nice touch to show me that. There's no need for you to get jealous."

"I know." He smiled, his annoyance at himself already gone. "If you're going to be spoiled this much, I will have to insist we eat together all the time because there's no way I'd get biscuits or a meal like this from the mess, even when I was here as Scrillia's son."

Zal made a series of appreciative noises as he attacked his food, reminding Devlin that the Chroalian way of showing they enjoyed a meal was to bolt it down as fast as possible.

Devlin was more careful with his food, taking his time to enjoy the individual pieces and mixing the ones with flavours he thought would do well together. How Zal managed to eat it all he had no idea, and he wanted to conserve some space for what he hoped would be dessert.

"Aren't you going to eat that?" Zal asked, staring at his plate.

"I don't want to get too full." The words had barely left his mouth as Zal speared something that reminded Devlin of a peppery yellow potato. "Please, go ahead and help yourself."

Zal grinned as he ate it. "You know what, Devlin? I didn't realise you were so unwilling to share."

"I'm willing to, but my company doesn't seem to appreciate my generosity."

Zal slid off his seat and onto his knees in front of him. Devlin swallowed as Zal stared up at him, his eyes now purple, showing he wanted something other than food, and he licked his lips. "How about I show you how grateful I am that you're willing to share your life with me?"

Zal slid his hands up Devlin's thighs. Devlin glanced at the door. "What if someone were to come in? Wouldn't the room be monitored somehow?"

"Shush, the room's booked, so no one should be able to get in without a high-level security code. As for monitoring, beyond the bioscans to confirm we're both in here, anything more would be highly intrusive."

"I..."

Zal paused, his hand on the fly of Devlin's trousers. "If you want me to stop I will."

"No, please don't."

The sound of his zip seemed abnormally loud. He lifted his hips to help Zal slide down his trousers and boxers so they pooled around his ankles. He bit his lip as Zal nuzzled his pubic hair. "I can't get enough of the way you smell and feel. You're so delectable."

Zal licked his cock from base to tip, and Devlin had to hold on to the arms of the chair to keep himself in his seat. He moaned, the deep reverberation echoing from his chest as Zal swallowed his cock, his shaft disappearing between Zal's perfect lips. When they'd been apart, his dreams had been haunted by such an image. He'd woken several times in a sweat of desire only to have dream Zal disappear and leave behind frustration and despair. But now here he was, worshipping Devlin's cock, down on his knees and making the most wonderful noises. Zal teased him with his tongue and then took him deep and hummed.

With a protracted shout, Devlin came, only vaguely aware Zal had his hand in his trousers, taking care of his own erection. Zal swallowed Devlin's release before sitting back on his heels and finishing himself off with his hand.

Devlin sank to his knees, pulling Zal to him and claiming a deep messy kiss. His heart was racing, his body singing, and if he hadn't been certain before that he'd made the right decision to leave Earth, he would have been now. They'd only been together on Earth a couple of weeks and had been apart for three months, so he knew they still had much to learn about each other. He knew there would be some people who'd think him mad to have left his planet, but he'd never get this sort of opportunity again, and to be able to explore the universe with Zal was beyond any dream. Zal's eyes were their vibrant post-orgasm yellow, and Devlin loved him with every fibre of his being.

Chapter Four

Devlin would have preferred to have woken up with Zal's tail wrapped around his middle, but they both knew that in order for things to work out for the best in the long term it was a necessity they slept apart. Maybe they were being overcautious, but Zal agreed they didn't want to risk his new position. If they did this right their relationship wouldn't be called into doubt, and then at the end of the two years of his placement, he could stay with Zal and not return to Earth.

There was no sunrise to wake him; instead the alarm he'd set had chimed and he slowly opened his eyes. Devlin knew he would need to adapt for what passed as a day on board, which was an interplanetary standard day-length equivalent to thirty hours split over three-thirds, representing morning, afternoon, and night. The climate programme mimicked the light to appear as morning.

Despite his longer day, it had taken more time than usual to get to sleep, the excitement of being aboard the ship, as well as knowing Zal was next door, plus the unfamiliar bed, meant it took him a while to drift off. The other thing keeping him awake was knowing he would be having breakfast with Zal's mother. True, he'd wanted to talk to her about ambassador duties, but he hadn't expected her to collar him so soon.

He got up, showered and dressed, and then realised he didn't know where, on the *Endeavour*, Scrillia's cabin or consulting rooms were. He thought it best to ask Zal and stared at the screen on the wall, wondering what to do. Tentatively, he tapped the screen and a green light flashed. "Er…can I speak to Zal Catenmir, please?"

The panel beeped. "Putting you through to cabin 223, Ambassador Taylor."

From what Zal had told him, he knew the ship had some sort of AI running many of its systems, but he wasn't sure how far it extended, and he would need Zal to explain. Zal appeared, bleary-eyed on the screen. "Morning, gorgeous," Devlin said with a grin. "Sleep well?"

"Devlin, it took me ages to get to sleep. I almost gave up and came over to you, but I know you'd have sent me back. Is there something wrong?"

"I had trouble sleeping too. There's nothing wrong. It's just I'm meant to be having breakfast with your mother, and I've no idea where to find her."

"Not that I mind you asking, but why didn't you just ask the ship's computer, like you did to call me?"

To be honest, the idea hadn't crossed his mind. "Oh, I suppose I should have thought of that. Sorry."

Zal smiled fondly at him. "It'll take some time to get used to things. Give me a few minutes, and I'll come and collect you."

Scrillia had been clear on it just being Devlin for breakfast, but he wouldn't stop Zal from tagging along. She could always send him away. "If you hurry, I might give you a good morning kiss to make it worth your while."

"I'll be straight over."

Devlin laughed as his screen went blank, and he barely had the chance to slip on his jacket and shoes when Zal sailed through his door, looking rumpled but demanding a kiss. "Give up those lips, Taylor. I've been cruelly separated for too long, and I'm not going to have you with me for whole stretches of the day, so I'll need something to get me through."

"You survived three months without my kisses," he said, but took Zal into his arms. "But I dare say I can give you something to ease the pain."

"I survived but I did not thrive."

"You sweet-talking bastard." He kissed him and shivered with delight as Zal's tail stroked his arse.

They broke apart. As much as he'd like to spend all day kissing Zal, he did have somewhere to be. Zal looked more than a little ragged. "Did you sleep in your clothes?"

"No, but I didn't take my time getting dressed. I wasn't about to miss out on those kisses."

"Well, now you've had them, you better tidy yourself up so we can go find your mum."

"She'd give me so much grief if I turned up like this. She'd make all sorts of comments. Honestly, when it comes to my love life, she thinks anything is fair game." Zal took several minutes to adjust his clothes, tucking in his shirt and making sure all his zips and buttons were fastened correctly.

Devlin wondered if this might be a good opportunity to bring up whatever it was that Zal and Holjin had shared, but he didn't have time and didn't want to start something they couldn't finish. Instead, he herded Zal out before he could be distracted by more kisses.

"I'll come and pry you away from her in a couple of hours; otherwise you'll be there all day," Zal said as they made their way to a level two decks up where Zal's parents were housed.

"I'm sure she won't be that bad. Besides, I can learn a lot from your mum, and while I'm with her I can avoid the captain and his wandering hands."

"That's true, but the longer you're with her unaccompanied, the higher the risk for baby pictures so it's a double-edged sword."

"I might ask for the pictures as an opening gambit."

"Don't you dare!"

When they stopped outside a door, Devlin wished he could lean in and kiss Zal, but he needed to be patient for just a couple of weeks, and then he could put his hands all over Zal whenever he wanted. The door slid open and Scrillia appeared. She was beautiful, although Devlin might be biased because she reminded him of her son. Her hair was half tied up and the rest ran long over her shoulders. "Ah, Zal, why did I get the feeling you'd be here even though I said I wanted to have breakfast just with Devlin?"

"I was showing him where your quarters were. Really, Mum, you're too suspicious for your own good."

"A likely story. But since I knew you'd turn up, I told your dad you'd be able to help him with an issue he's had with the ship's computer." Her smile and Zal's pout told Devlin that Zal had been rumbled. "It won't take you long, but I'm sure he'll appreciate your help."

Devlin's parents hadn't lived long enough for him to have to deal with their computer problems, but he'd heard his team moan about the woes of trying to help elderly parents, so he didn't envy Zal, even if somehow he'd expected Dharl not to have issues with technology.

Scrillia slipped her arm into his. "I've arranged for breakfast to be delivered to my consulting rooms. I thought you wouldn't want to be on display in the mess quite yet. You can work up to that."

Zal made a huffing noise that signified he knew he was beaten. "I'll see you later?" Devlin asked.

"I'll come by and pick you up for lunch, to give you a break from my mother."

"Don't be surprised if you need to change your plans. I've already heard from Captain Holjin asking when Devlin might be free."

"Why is he asking you and not me?" Zal huffed. "I'm Devlin's liaison."

She raised an eyebrow. "I don't think there's anything nefarious about it. He contacted me to request I spend some time with Devlin, and I simply told him I was meeting with him already."

"He didn't need to contact you about that either."

Devlin wondered what had triggered the reaction. "Surely it's better the captain of the ship is taking a positive interest. If he didn't want me here, it would have made the ambassador opportunity nigh on impossible."

"Absolutely," said Scrillia. "Zal is just feeling a little territorial, that's all. Come on, Devlin."

They left Zal muttering under his breath, Devlin tried to give him an encouraging look but Zal was disgruntled over something, and he'd deal with that later. Zal's reaction had made him more determined to talk to Scrillia. Her consulting rooms were on the same level but on the opposite side. There was a teapot on the table.

"I thought it would be a nice gesture to share some tea at our first meeting. It's from the collection the captain arranged, and I found brewing instructions." She held up a little jug. "We have something similar to milk, so I hope it does the job."

He was charmed by the action and watched as she filled two

cups. He took a sip. "Delicious. Thank you. I appreciate the thought."

"I think," she said, sitting opposite, "it would be good to get the conversations about Zal and your relationship out of the way first, then we can concentrate on how I can guide you on your new role."

She had a directness about her that he hadn't expected. From what he'd seen on Earth her style was more consolatory and bridging than direct. "If you're going to tell me not to break your little boy's heart, I think leaving my home planet should be enough to show how serious I am about him."

She sipped her drink, her expression one of pleasant surprise, but she didn't comment on it. "Zal is a grown man. I try not to get embroiled in his romantic liaisons unless I have to. Having said that, I'd have happily bashed his ex-partner, the smug Telgan, across the head with his own framed diploma—not that it would have solved anything."

"Then what do we need to get out of the way?"

"Zal isn't normally the type to get so jealous. I can honestly say I have never seen him act as he has done about you and Holjin."

"I had intended to ask about what was going on there. Obviously, I will speak to Zal, but I got the impression something has rubbed him up the wrong way, and he's actually more upset about his own reaction than anything the captain might have done."

"Now I see why you impressed so many aliens you helped

settle on Earth. There's not many who would be so perceptive."

She was giving him too much credit. Zal wasn't the hardest person to read, and even in the short time he'd known him, he could see the different aspects of body language at play. "Look, if Zal had a fling with Holjin, that's not an issue for me. I can imagine when he returned from Earth he was at a low ebb, and it would have been natural to find comfort with someone."

"Oh, it didn't happen then. Zal's tryst with the captain happened when he first came aboard the *Endeavour* after breaking up with Telgan. He was in no mood for anyone else after you, and I didn't mean to lead you to that conclusion."

Devlin was more confused. "Then if it's not because he thinks I'll be upset, what's it about? He can't possibly think I'm interested in the captain when I've spent three months pining away and then, as near as damn it, eloped with him."

"Not seriously, that's why he's so annoyed with himself. The captain is an attractive man, and there's many who've enjoyed the pleasure of his company. Plus, Chroalians don't generally judge someone with a higher than average appetite for sex, and are more affectionate and tactile than many other species."

"So he's annoyed at himself for being annoyed at himself. That seems a bit self-defeating?"

"It's not rational; that's for sure."

Devlin made a quiet humming noise. "I'm going to tackle this head-on. I don't want it festering, and I want him to understand that I'm here to support him, not just the other way around."

Scrillia smiled at that. "I get the sense that he can't quite believe he's managed to get what he wanted. He's a brilliant researcher and this ship, and its mission, will only help his career. But the real prize is having you with him. My baby is in love, and not the pale imitation he thought he had with his ex."

"He gave me his earring when he left Earth. But I gave it back. Should I have done?"

She bit her lip. "We usually exchange earrings to signify the start of a courtship. He wouldn't have given it to you if he didn't want you to have it, but at the same time he didn't think he would see you again."

Devlin knew this—Zal had told him—but he still couldn't shake that Zal would have preferred for him to have kept it. "He told me when I came aboard that he wanted to court me properly, but maybe I've given him the wrong impression by returning the earring."

She clapped her hands together in delight. "Court you! Oh, Devlin, I can barely believe it. Zal has never been one for the old traditions but it seems you've brought out a different side of him. That is wonderful. And do not worry about the earring, I'm pretty sure you'll be getting it back sooner rather than later."

He hadn't been expecting such a response, thinking more along the lines of a parent being cautious about rushing things, although it wasn't as if Devlin could do a moonlight flit. "I thought the concept would be similar to marriage on Earth."

"The endgame is, but we like to take a scenic route and

celebrate on the way." Her eyes shone and he was a little worried about how involved this might be. "I won't spoil it for you, but I promise, if done right, you'll be thoroughly charmed."

"Okay." By the sound of it, Zal had started his plan the night before in the viewing bubble, a sort of stealth kick-off to their courtship, although he had said he was from a region known for being romantic, so he would need to learn more about Zal's home planet.

Scrillia chuckled and topped up his tea. "Don't look so worried, I have no intention of interfering. If he talks to anyone—and I'm not convinced he will—it'll be his dad, not me."

Devlin didn't think that was more reassuring, but he supposed it was better his boyfriend's parents were supportive, especially how fast their romance had blossomed. "I'll leave that to Zal. I wouldn't want to ruin his fun."

"Indeed not. Besides, you'll be plenty busy trying to find your feet on this ship. You've taken on quite a challenge, you realise?"

He had a vague idea, but he knew he was woefully unprepared. The speed at which he'd gone from being confirmed as ambassador, to joining the crew, was only a matter of days. Zal had been a great help but there was much he was going to have to learn and fast. "I did have a head start from the files we received as part of the Chroalian visit to Earth, and it's not like I've not been around aliens for the last decade or so."

"Yes, but you'll have experienced aliens who were either after help and wished to settle on Earth, or wanted to help Earth like the Chroalians. You've probably not encountered anyone hostile, or even indifferent. There are a lot of species who I am afraid will think you are insignificant or your existence is beneath them."

"I've dated worse," he replied, with a wry smile.

"Devlin, be serious," she replied, but she was smirking. "I don't doubt you can handle yourself in terms of diplomacy, but some firearms training and self-defence sessions wouldn't hurt."

"I was in active service for several years, which means running down any undesirables that came to Earth uninvited. I might be rusty, but I can still defend myself." Chroalian weaponry would be different though, and that did give him pause. "If I were to be armed, then a crash course on what passes for handguns wouldn't go amiss."

She picked up her tablet device. "I think that would be the minimum. I put together a few things that I thought you should consider, and I have discussed them with Captain Holjin. He was very keen to provide some training personally, if you think it appropriate."

"We'll be meeting later. I'll see what he has in mind, and if it's more physical contact than I think Zal's sensibilities can handle, then I'll see if he can recommend someone else."

"Zal's sensibilities should not be put before your safety. Holjin is the best shot on the ship and more patient than his general demeanour would suggest."

It was clear she wasn't used to being argued with, but also evident that she had his best intentions at heart. "If the captain can find the time, then I'll bear it in mind."

He didn't think she would push his need for training further now, but he got the sense that this wasn't negotiable. It wasn't as if he was totally defenceless, but he would admit the equipment he would have used on Earth was projectile-based and from the snatches he'd seen aboard ship, bullets were not the order of the day.

"Right, back to my list. I know Zal will see you well for the general operations aboard, but there are people you should know from a personal standpoint. You're the only human, but there are a few non-Chroalians and I think you'd appreciate having some-one who can empathise with your position."

Zal had mentioned them but he hadn't had details, so he would spend some time reading that part of Scrillia's notes. "Agreed."

"Then there's the senior bridge crew, who are a must. Addi-tionally, the ship's chef is well versed in the cuisine of multiple species, and I can tell you there's nothing that breaks the ice in diplomatic talks than being able to bond over food. And he does love to bake—as you saw by the biscuits. There are several re-searchers whose fields of study are diverse, and knowing the gap between ours and the Earth's technology will help you gauge how advanced a species is."

"Daresay the Earth would not be on the top of the list for a technology exchange. While I have information of potential trad-ing opportunities such as ores and metals, I believe we'll be seen as having a begging bowl out."

"I knew you were more astute than the average politician," she said with a conspiratorial wink. "You're spot on, but there were others from your Ministry that were completely blinkered by the idea that other species would be falling over themselves to liaise with Earth. You can't go out there and offer much of anything; you'll be trading on your lovely personality."

"Oh dear. Sounds like the Earth's screwed."

"Screwed? Not sure my translator picked that up correctly. It seems to think it's an expletive but could also be something holding pieces of wood together?"

"Apologies, I need to remember to choose my words better. Less colloquialisms will help everyone, I think." He bit down on his laugh. There was a time and a place and this wasn't it. "The level of translation into English is generally such good quality, it's easy to forget that we're speaking different languages."

"Brings me nicely to another topic. I would suggest trying to learn some Chroalian. The translator will do most of the work but they are not perfect, and there's something nice about hearing and understanding your partner speaking their own language."

He'd heard snippets of Zal speak what he thought was Chroalian, and he had to admit Scrillia was right. "I was pretty good at languages. I speak three Earth languages, not fluently, by any means, but more than just getting by. But I think I need to start further back, including the real basics of what the letters are." That's how he'd learnt Russian.

"I've found a few words of the language of the species you are making contact with makes all the difference. The translator will also modulate your speech, it might only be a fractional change, but there will always be a slight difference so you're missing out on hearing the true cadence of someone's tone."

He wondered how different Zal sounded, the Chroalian words he'd heard from Zal were no doubt swear words but he'd love to hear more.

"How easy do you think it would be for me to learn Chroalian?"

"It's a matter of how much you want to learn it. There are computer simulations, and once you get to a certain level you could find someone who would be willing to practise." She tapped something into her tablet. "I've asked the computer to set up a beginners course for you. Start by doing a little every day, and it will come. Most people expect miracles to happen, but I'm afraid it doesn't work like that."

He knew what to expect, but at least his brain was receptive to other languages. He'd met enough humans, notably his fellow Brits, whose language expansion went no further than trying to pronounce something off an Italian menu. "I'll make it part of my daily schedule. I'll need something to do."

She scoffed. "You won't be lacking for things to do, Devlin. Getting used to being here and learning Chroalian is just the start, and since Earth already has a relationship with us, it's the rest of the universe you need to convince."

"I was hoping to have a little time to settle in before I met the whole universe. There is only so much of me to go around."

She laughed and patted his hand. "Bless you. I suppose you won't want to hear you have four days before we enter orbit for our next planetary visit."

"What?" He must have heard that wrong. But then no one had given him a detailed itinerary beyond that it would take ten months to reach Chroalia, so it was his own fault for not asking.

"We're on a voyage of diplomacy and discovery, meaning we have a schedule of visits planned."

"I knew that. I just thought the first would happen a little later." His desperation to be with Zal had caused him to overlook this, so he would need to be careful that nothing else would slip past him. "I need the schedule and, of course, details of what's coming first."

"If you aren't ready, you can stay on the ship," she said kindly. "Zal used to do that or just take part in sample collection."

"No, I didn't leave Earth to hide in my cabin. I admit I took the role to be with Zal, but I intend to do the job to the best of my ability. He doesn't need to babysit me all the time, and we don't need to be in each other's pockets."

"I am glad to hear it." From a panel in her chair, she removed a tablet similar to her own. "I have prepared a few items that you might find useful. Just to make it clear, I never doubted your capability, or your commitment to Zal, but to the ambassador position remains to be seen."

Devlin bristled at the slight against his professionalism, but he knew this wasn't the time to argue. Nice words wouldn't work here. He would need to demonstrate what he could do and earn his spurs as if he were a pioneer in the Wild West. In a small way he was—he was charting new territory for humans, and although he wasn't travelling on the wagon train, and he wasn't likely to die of cholera, that wasn't to say something a little more exotic wouldn't get him.

"I'm confident that I'm more than up for the job. You might have applied a certain leverage, but my management wouldn't have assigned me if they didn't think me capable, and they did not know of my relationship with Zal."

Her eyes twinkled and she wore an expression similar to the one Zal pulled when he was contemplating something but wasn't ready to share. "Let's begin on a few basic meet-and-greet topics. I'm sure you'll know it all already."

Chapter Five

Zal watched with amusement as Chief Science Officer Lian lifted his head off his desk with a pained groan. "Zal, thank the lords. I thought you were Ghisle. I can't cope with another lab accident today."

"Ghisle's not that bad." That wasn't true. She was a complete disaster, and he'd refused point-blank to have her on his team. He'd known her from his student days, when she'd managed to ignore the lab safety guidelines and pour random chemicals down the sink to get rid of them, causing a mushroom cloud of smoke to rise from the drain. From what he'd witnessed, she hadn't got any better. "Anyway, I've just popped in to pick up a few files and check in on a couple of experiments, but I'll be with the Earth Ambassador most of the week."

"He seems like a decent individual. Might be interesting to

see how long he manages to keep Holjin's paws off him, but Ambassador Taylor doesn't seem the type to have his head turned easily, which will be important in his role."

He held back his response that the captain would never get his paws on Devlin. "I spent some time with him on Earth when I visited as part of the diplomatic mission. From what I saw, he was the best candidate. He had a way of putting people at ease."

Lian raised an eyebrow. "Appears that it's not just the captain who's got an interest in Devlin Taylor."

"I'm his liaison," Zal said, trying to sound outraged.

"For now, but we'll see." Lian had a way of knowing things that made Zal wonder if he should have been trained for the Sentinel League. "You won't be the only one who'd be interested in knowing what it would be like to bed a human, so you'd best not hang around, as you'll have some fierce competition."

Zal knew this, but he hadn't expected his immediate supervisor to point it out and spur him on. "He does have pretty eyes. They're a colour Chroalians don't have, a greeny-browny hazel colour."

"I heard human males are furry too. Not overly, like a full pelt, but a fine layer that I must say is quite intriguing from an evolutionary standpoint."

Zal didn't want to get into an academic discussion on human physiology, nor did he want to let slip that he knew first-hand more than probably any other Chroalian alive. "Yeah, according to the information we received, many of the men have body hair. I tell you what, in the unlikely event I find out, I'll let you know if it's true."

"Someone will find out and Devlin's furriness will be the subject of ship gossip for weeks. You weren't on board when the Vengrasian was with us for a month, but half the ship wanted to know what colour their skin turned when they orgasmed."

Zal bit back his response of *blue*, since Lian didn't need to know that Zal had found that out after a rowdy evening on a space station when he was celebrating a friend getting a new research grant. They'd been fun times, but he didn't miss them, not now he had Devlin.

"I'd best get going. Is Teric in? I wanted to see if she could cover a couple of things for me."

"She should be. Try the light lab. She was attempting a new scanning technique. Approach with caution—I don't think it was going too well."

He left Lian to his headaches over his staff and went in search of Teric. He found her muttering darkly over a set of scans that were more smears than anything else. "I think you might have a little resolution problem there."

She stared at him and gave him a very rude three-fingered salute. "What do you want? I thought you'd be cock deep in your human boy toy this week."

"Oi, his name is Devlin." Teric was one of the few aboard the *Endeavour* who knew about his and Devlin's relationship. "And he's an ambassador, not my boy toy. Technically, he's the equivalent of a few cycles older than me."

"Yes, yes, whatever. It still doesn't explain why you're in here annoying me instead of being joined hip to tail with him."

She struggled to remove her safety goggles, the elastic strap tangling in her long silver hair. Zal came to her aid and helped free her before she ripped out a hank of hair in frustration. "Wanna go for a quick break?" he asked.

"All right, beats staring at this shit."

He laughed as she threw the goggles hard against the bench in retaliation and deleted images of the scan. "It's not that bad; at least you're getting smears. It's just a matter of tweaking from here on in."

"Why are you so fucking cheerful?"

Zal smirked and flicked his tail suggestively.

"Fucking couples," she said, rolling her eyes.

"Quite literally, but I think I'm allowed to be smug considering the three months before when I was miserable and broken-hearted."

She huffed. She'd put up with a lot of his moping. "Don't I know it. Come on, I fancy a litha tea. I think I need the spice to clear my head. Everything I've touched recently has gone to shit."

They left the lab. "We all have runs like that. I nearly lost a grant when one project failed to yield results, and it was only a chance sample I took on a whim that saved it."

He'd ended up having a heart-to-heart with a fellow academic on his issues, that being with Telgan, and one thing had led to another, resulting in a long-term relationship that had been deeply unsatisfying in the end. He shook away the annoyance; Telgan was his past now, and he was surprised how easy it was to shake off the anger, which even a couple of months before, would have left him frustrated and bitching. Devlin had a lot to do with that, but it wasn't just him. Zal had found a new peace within himself.

The mess was quiet, only a handful of folks enjoying a late breakfast, and that suited Zal perfectly. Teric bagged their favourite table in the corner by a porthole and Zal collected their drinks from an automated dispenser and grabbed a couple of the chewy sweet snacks he liked but was rarely lucky enough to get. Teric had her head on her arms when he got back to her, and she looked thoroughly miserable. "Come on, it can't be that bad."

"It's not just work," she admitted. "Jils wants to call it quits, and I thought we were getting on great."

He wracked his brain to remember who Jils was. Teric had a different girlfriend most months, but he didn't remember this one. "Which one's she?"

"From engineering, lateral flow specialist. She has long wonderfully callused fingers." She let out a dreamy sigh. "I've not introduced you. We only got together the night you left to bring back your human."

"I've probably seen her around somewhere if she's in engineering. Us tech folks tend to stick together." Teric seemed to be turning on the dramatics for someone who sounded like an extended one-night stand. "It's not like you to be bothered this quickly."

"I'm not sure I'm bothered about her in particular, more an ego thing that she's not that bothered by me." She sat up properly. "Ah, well, no use moping. There's plenty of other options on the ship. There's the pretty lady from Merrus… Wouldn't mind seeing if her tattoos are all over her body."

Teric was good at bouncing back. "No shortage if you're looking."

"It's all right for you; you're not still out there searching for Mr Perfect. You've already found yours, lassoed him, and dragged him back to your cabin for lots of filthy interspecies sex."

He glanced around, relieved their table was still out of earshot of anyone else. "I don't want to know what porn you've been watching, but I'm pretty sure the sex you've had was a lot more filthy than mine." And that was if the stories were only half true, even accounting for what he'd got up to when he was younger. "Devlin is fantastic, and I'm sure it won't take long for the rest of the crew to think the same too."

"Then you'd better hurry up and stake your claim. I noticed you've your earring back…"

She knew the story and what he'd done. "If anyone asks, I lost it on Earth and Devlin found it and gave it back, not that I gave it to him in the first place."

She gnawed her lip. "So you're not courting?"

"Not officially. We're not anything at the moment until we

can find the right time to announce we're a couple."

"So does that include you not minding the idea of him trying out a few other Chroalians to reassure himself he's already got the best one?"

His growl was involuntary. "Devlin's mine."

"I didn't say he wasn't. But are you saying he's done something to make you think he's not? Like giving back the earring?"

"No!"

"Oh, so where's the comments coming from about the crew finding out about him being special?" She pursed her lips. "Do you think he'll find someone else now he's here? If so, Zal, you know that'll make you sound like a gilmit's arsehole? This guy left his planet for you and has done nothing to make you doubt him, so suggesting he's going to fuck himself around the ship is pretty out of order."

He had no idea why she'd jumped to that conclusion. He'd admit he was sensitive over Captain Holjin, but he had no concerns about Devlin falling for anyone else on the crew.

"Devlin's not like that, and I know I've nothing to worry about. But there are others on the ship that aren't shy in trying to put their sticky fingers on anything."

She groaned. "Is this about Holjin again? I thought you'd got over that."

"There wasn't anything to get over. It was one night which I should have known better to do in the first place. I had my tail turned, but I've no interest in anything more."

"Yeah, I know; that wasn't what I meant."

He'd been disappointed in himself after sleeping with the captain. The night itself had been fun, and the sex enjoyable—not a patch on Devlin, but then Devlin had the fuzziness. He'd tried to find self-affirmation after his break-up with Telgan in the wrong way. Then he'd almost done something as foolish when he'd gone clubbing on Earth.

"I still feel a bit stupid. I didn't exactly act my intelligence when I was on Earth either."

She seemed surprised at that. "But then you wouldn't have Devlin, and I've never seen you so happy. You can't be having regrets already."

"Oh no, not about Devlin. It's just that I nearly ballsed it all up in some misguided idea that I just wanted a bit of fun so went out looking for someone to have fun with." His stomach squirmed at the memory. "I'd already slept with Devlin, and I had some stupid idea in my head that what I needed to do was go out and be like I was when I was younger."

"Oh no, not Cock Slut Zal."

"Oi, I was never that bad."

"Please, you collected more men than samples." She laughed. "No one cares, especially not me with my own collection, but I did think that was well in the past, seeing how you reacted after you joined the ship and realised Brilli was on board with Appla."

They were something different, and another link back to his

youth that he'd need to at least mention to Devlin—soon.

"Nothing happened. I'd already developed a soft spot for Devlin, and I was desperate for it not to get worse since I didn't think I'd ever see him again after we left Earth. Instead, he'd followed me to the club, and saw me dancing up close and personal with someone else."

"I take it that didn't go down well."

"No, but not in the sense that you mean. I hadn't been honest with him. I had ditched my tracker and snuck out. He was assigned to look after me and had protocols to follow to ensure I was safe. I acted like an idiot." He remembered the look of hurt Devlin had tried to disguise; he'd even tried to apologise for interrupting. "We talked and decided to enjoy the time we had left together. I'm fucking lucky Devlin's one of the good guys."

"He does sound like he's a keeper. I take it he knows about Holjin."

"We haven't discussed it. Holjin opened his big mouth and implied something had gone on. Devlin's too bright not to have noticed."

"Then you better speak to him, and while you're at it, you might want to be a bit more honest about your past as well. Not that it's really his business, but the diplomatic and research circles can be a bit small, and you're bound to run into a few of your conquests. And whatever it was you had going on with Brilli and his now bond-mate."

She had a point. It wasn't that he hadn't told Devlin that he'd been wilder when he was younger, but he hadn't been transparent on how wild. "Yeah, you're right."

"People will try to lure Devlin from you, but you need to remember not to transfer what you did when you first left Chroalia onto Devlin." She sipped her tea and stared at him over the rim of the cup. "Which would be a pretty shitty thing to do."

This is why he had needed to speak to her, she knew when he needed to hear the truth, keep him honest and not sugar-coat it. His mum might say something that meant the same, but it was Teric's bluntness that made the difference. "I can always rely on you to give me the kick up the tail when I need it."

"You're so lucky, Zal. You've both taken a really big chance on each other; you owe it to yourselves not to mess it up."

Zal didn't expect Devlin to have any issues with his past—he wasn't the type. But he needed to be honest, and that applied to any topic. What he needed to do was be open about his own history and how he'd been more than a little wild compared to human standards, and reassure Devlin that he had no interest in anyone else.

Chapter Six

Devlin's head was full. If Scrillia tried to impart any more knowledge, he was sure it would explode. He hoped Zal would be here soon to save him from his mum. A chirping noise made Scrillia look up from her notes. "Ah, is that the time already? I fear we've much still to cover, so same time tomorrow, and we'll put in a reoccurring meeting."

He should have known that even going into space meant he wouldn't be able to escape attending meetings. At least Scrillia provided a close approximation of decent coffee after they'd finished their tea.

She instructed the door to open, but where he'd expected to see Zal was Captain Holjin. There was no mistaking that Holjin was an attractive man, and from his swagger, he knew it as well. He held himself in a way that probably only the captain of a spaceship could, full of expectation that everyone would do exactly what he would say.

"Scrillia, I've come to steal Devlin away from you."

Scrillia stood and Devlin followed. "I'm sure Devlin will be relieved by the change of pace."

She wasn't wrong, but also he'd been hoping for a little downtime with Zal before seeing the captain. Holjin might bring a change of content but he still had to be as focused. "Thank you for your time, Scrillia. You probably had much more important things to do than spending your morning with me."

"Nonsense. It's been a most rewarding morning, and I look forward to doing so again tomorrow."

Holjin smiled. "I hope we can have an equally pleasurable session together. I'm keen to help foster a special relationship between Earth and Chroalia. Shall we go?"

He could hardly say no and, if nothing else, it was good to stretch his legs as he'd been sitting for the best part of three hours, so he followed Holjin out of Scrillia's consulting rooms.

"How was your first night aboard a starship? I hope your cabin was comfortable and that you're not feeling too homesick for Earth. I don't want you getting lonely. You're among people you don't know, with none of your own species."

"I'm sure I won't be lonely. There's many people on the *Endeavour* and everyone has been very friendly."

Holjin squeezed his shoulder. "You're a brave man, Devlin. There's not many who would leave everything behind. You're doing a great service for humanity."

"We'll see about that. I've yet to visit my first planet. I might start some sort of conflict and get Earth a terrible reputation."

They entered the lift. "You can only improve the Earth's reputation. Humans aren't exactly considered the most advanced race in the galaxy."

"Of course not, but we can't be so bad."

Holjin seemed surprised by his answer. "You're not considered that good though. Otherwise you wouldn't be limited by the accords."

"That's because we weren't ready." Although the words didn't sound as convincing as he thought they should.

"You're improving. But I don't think you should expect the average human to be allowed free travel any time soon."

"The average human isn't even aware alien life exists. But that doesn't mean a select few shouldn't be out here building a future for when we will be ready." He could imagine the panic if a normal Londoner were to realise their neighbour wasn't from Swindon or Aberdeen but from a solar system they probably couldn't even pronounce, let alone find on an astronomy map.

"With no central government and intermittent conflict breaking out on a regular basis, I think knowing about aliens isn't the biggest challenge you're going to have as a species to get the accords fully disassembled."

He couldn't argue with the logic; humans must look like troglodytes to a species such as the Chroalians. "We have to start somewhere. And we can't all be that bad; otherwise why would the Chroalians support my tenancy aboard this ship."

"Oh, you're definitely not all bad." Holjin flashed him a sexy grin. If he didn't have Zal, he might have been tempted to reciprocate, but without Zal he wouldn't be here in the first place. "But helping species like humans is part of our continuing mission."

"I thought this was a research vessel, and you were escorting Ambassador Scrillia more out of being in the right place, rather than by design."

"There are research vessels in the fleet that only have a single purpose, but the *Endeavour* is fitted out with not only the best scientific facilities but also weapons and tactical capabilities well above the usual for a ship in her class."

Devlin was surprised to hear that. "Are you expecting trouble? I got the impression this was a peaceful mission, travelling through areas of space without known threats."

"I'm not sure such a place exists outside our solar system, and that wouldn't be the most exciting of diplomatic missions. Pretty much like Earth, Chroalia is the only inhabited planet that orbits our sun."

Zal had given him the history of Chroalian space exploration, although at quite a high level, so he had thought that the Chroalians and humans had several parallels on how they had reached the stars. Including support from a far more advanced race called the Atrachi. "Chroalia and Earth's first journey beyond their solar systems are similar. As you are helping us, the Atrachi helped you."

"Yes and no. We were much more advanced, technologically speaking. The Atrachi had seen our experiments and offered us not the means on how to travel, but guidance on how we could put our theories into action, and who we might encounter when we did."

There was something about the way he said it that gave Devlin pause. Zal had sung the Atrachi's praises when they discussed his peoples' history and called them Chroalia's greatest friend and ally, but Holjin sounded much more reserved. "I was told how important their help was."

"Of that there is no dispute, but you do need to remember that friends will always have an opinion on who else you will talk to and influence what it is you might say."

Now that was an interesting turn of phrase, and he was about to press further when they reached a door which slid open to reveal the bridge. The front area was taken up by a huge window, which he was pretty sure would have a more technical name, but to him it was exactly what it was, and it gave the most stunning view of the expanse of stars before them. On either side and extending down both walls were banks of touchscreen monitors, bigger versions of the panel in his cabins, with schematics and controls, and several crew members watching the contents.

The captain's chair sat in the middle, and slightly behind it was a console with two other Chroalians, one he recognised from the evening before, the second a woman with jet-black hair, he didn't. "Devlin, let me introduce you to Commander Sihil, my second in command and the reason this ship runs so smoothly."

There was great affection in his voice, with no sexual undertone. This woman had a very different place in Holjin's estimations than a fleeting encounter would earn. She stood, and he could see her strength in her wiry frame—even her tail looked powerful. "Welcome aboard, Ambassador Taylor. Apologies, I was not able to attend your welcome event, but someone had to keep the ship on course."

He held up his hand in greeting, and she pressed her palm to his. "My pleasure to meet you. Please call me Devlin."

"I hope you do not mind, Devlin," began Holjin, "but I have asked Sihil to give you a few lessons on firearms and combat skills. I know that in general, an ambassador is not a military position, but I do feel you should be able to defend yourself. I had thought to offer myself, but I have competing priorities, so perhaps an advanced session in a few weeks."

Scrillia had mentioned the option as well, and again he couldn't help but think there was more to this than met the eye. "You'll be glad to hear I'm not a complete novice, but I, of course, will be honoured to learn the Chroalian way of doing things."

"That is intriguing. In our first session, I will take a measure of your capabilities. You never know when you might end up in combat."

He had no doubt she could fell him in a single blow if he wasn't prepared, but this was not a threat, only a genuine desire to see if he could protect himself. "I've found myself in such a situation more than once. I hope that if I can defend myself, I might be in a position to help defend others. I don't intend to be a burden to the crew of the *Endeavor*."

Sihil grinned. "I am glad to hear it. We have had the pleasure of escorting many diplomats over the years, and you will be a rarity if you live up to your claims."

He returned the grin. "If you wish to see my service record, I'd be happy to provide it."

"No need. You can't get a true measure of a man's capabilities from a report."

Holjin chuckled. "Now isn't that the truth. Come with me, Devlin. We can talk more in my ready room. I'd like to cover a few aspects of our mission and our next destination."

"I'll contact you later to arrange a time," said Sihil. "I'll let Zal know, as well. He was pretty insistent that he should know your schedule."

Holjin rolled his eyes. "Zal is Devlin's liaison, not his keeper. Devlin is not one of his lab team; he doesn't need Zal to lead him by the tail."

"I don't have a tail. Zal is only trying to ensure I settle into my life as easily as possible."

"I did wonder about the tail," said Holjin smirking, his own tail now writhing, and Devlin knew that if it was anything like Zal's, then Holjin's thoughts were not limited to the tail itself. "You could say I'm intrigued about many facets of human anatomy."

Sihil snorted. "Captain, you should take your leave."

He followed Holjin to a room off the side of the bridge that was a sort of office without a desk. There were a couple of two-seater sofas, a low table in the corner and a wall of monitors that he thought might be where Holjin probably held regular 1:1 briefings with members of his senior team. "Please take a seat. How about a drink? I've a very pleasing fruit infusion you might enjoy, I'm afraid I don't allow intoxicating substances anywhere near the bridge."

"I'd be concerned if you did. Drunk in charge of a starship isn't the sort of accolade someone would want following them about."

Devlin sat and accepted the drink which Holjin poured from a flask that was in a cabinet on the far wall, next to a mix of awards and firearms.

He wasn't surprised that instead of the other sofa, Holjin chose to sit next to him and place a tablet on the low table in front of them. On its screen was what looked to Devlin's uneducated eyes as a star chart. "Right, this is our current itinerary. I'll ensure you have a copy, plus my additional notes, which I think may help bring you up to speed a bit quicker than any official record."

"Thanks, that will be very useful. I understand our first destination is in four days. I'll admit I'm a little under-prepared, but I'll catch up."

"We're meeting the Xoroans, not our first visit with them, and they have some interesting agricultural technology." He expanded the map on the tablet and brought up the planet. "They fit nicely into our overarching mission, which in basic terms, is to encourage civilisations advanced enough for space travel to do so under a flag of peaceful cooperation."

"That's the Chroalian mission? How did Earth fit into that?"

"Not just Chroalia's, but the Union of Planets, the people behind the accords, and the mission has a branch objective to help promising species get to the point where they are advanced enough for space exploration."

The UoP weren't the most forthcoming about information about themselves. "They've not exactly given me a lot of insight."

Holjin laughed. "Well, not too surprising as Earth isn't a member. I'll arrange for you to get access and the right computer clearance, but you don't have to know everything straight away, and if you have any questions, I'm happy to make myself available. At any time."

Holjin squeezed his thigh but removed his hand to bring up more information about the Xoroans. "As you can see, we have a lot of information for you to process, Scrillia will ensure you know what you need to, and because there is a large xenobiological component, Zal will be leading the scientific team."

"Oh well, at least I'll be in safe hands there."

"Definitely. Zal's brilliant at what he does. But I do have to ask how you are getting on with him as your liaison. He's not taken a similar role before."

"Excellent. We got on very well when he was on Earth, and

he's been generous with his time and interest since I joined the crew. I couldn't be happier."

Holjin smirked. "Good to hear. He's not a tactical man though, so you'll stick close to me while we're down there for your own protection. I must insist that you have at least one session with Sihil, like we mentioned, or I'll revoke your permission to go down on me."

"I think the expression you mean is go down to the planet *with* you."

Holjin's eyes were turning purple, and Devlin guessed his choice of words was deliberate. "I do hope I did not mistranslate something."

"Nothing too bad but, as is the case in the Chroalian language I'm sure, a slight misalignment can easily conjure up different connotations."

He leant in closer. "I read that human eyes don't change colour. Does that mean their colour is not an obvious indicator of your mood?"

"There are plenty of other ways to gauge our mood."

"You smell different as well. I don't know if it's a perfume you are wearing or natural human excretion but it smells—" He licked his lips. "—divine."

Devlin took the opportunity to slide away to pick up his drink and put a little more distance between them, although it was a small sofa. "I would suggest that it's merely the effect of me being a new species to you. I wouldn't say I smell particularly alluring."

"It's not just your smell, Devlin. I'm very intrigued to find out about your lack of scales, and I read that male humans have quite a lot of body hair."

"Captain, I am not sure this conversation would be something I would be comfortable continuing."

"Oh come now, Devlin. We're both men of the universe; there's nothing wrong with experiencing new things." He slid his hand onto Devlin's thigh. "If you are willing, I'd be more than happy to show you a prime specimen of a Chroalia male."

"I don't doubt that, but it's hardly the diplomatic briefing my employer had in mind." Part of Devlin wondered if he should play along a bit more or if he should cut this off at the legs. He wanted to keep Holjin on his side for now, but he wasn't going to cross the line of something Zal wouldn't approve of.

"I'm keen to ensure diplomatic relations can be as enjoyable as possible. I'm positive we can explore a special interaction between our people."

"You're being very presumptuous, Captain."

"Am I?

A siren wailed suddenly and the ship's lights flashed to red. Holjin was on his feet in moments, his demeanour completely changed from lothario to protector of his ship.

"What's going on?" asked Devlin.

"The highest level security alert has been triggered." Holjin strode out of his ready room, and back to the bridge. Devlin decided to follow, wanting to know what was going on.

"Report!" Holjin demanded.

Sihil's fingers were dancing over several screens. "There appears to be an energy discharge—the computer has identified five lifeforms."

"Species?"

"Undetected. The scans are being blocked from using identification sub-routines, and the ship's cameras in the area have been disabled. We've a security detail on route to get visuals, Captain."

Devlin had to admit that Holjin in full captain mode was extremely dashing. He reeled off several orders that Devlin assumed were protocol and his senior crew were disciplined and experienced enough to do exactly as they were told. The view screen flickered into life, revealing five individuals who, if Devlin had to describe them, he'd say looked elvish. They had graceful features, high cheekbones and pointy ears, with long hair gathered in various braids, and wore leather, lots of leather; it couldn't be practical.

Having spent a large portion of his teens reading fantasy novels, he had come to the conclusion that Earth elves were arseholes and, by the looks of it, the space versions weren't any better.

"Any sign of a vessel?" Holjin asked.

"Working on it" Sihil replied. "There's nothing in range of our scanners."

"Then how did they get aboard?"

Devlin hadn't come across these particular aliens, but Earth had received several visitors over the years who had hidden their spacecrafts from Earth's detectors. "Can you modify your scanners?" he asked. "You've probably already got this covered, but we found using rapid pulses across multiple frequencies allowed us to pick up various cloaked vessels in orbit. Sometimes the scan only picked up a shadow, but it was enough to pinpoint an uninvited guest."

"Tactical Officer Schee, is that one of the protocols?" Holjin asked, flashing an impressed grin in Devlin's direction.

"Sort of, it's a mix of a couple of them," answered a squat individual from the back of the bridge. "I'm reconfiguring to an approximation of Ambassador Taylor's proposal. Give me a moment."

Holjin turned back to Sihil. "Do we have a species confirmation yet?"

"No, sir."

It seemed that elves weren't real in space either. But it was surprising that the Chroalians hadn't seen this species before. Of all the aliens he'd dealt with, they were some of the best connected and furthest-travelled.

"They appear to be on the move. But not towards the armoury or research. I think they're trying to reach the bridge."

A group of Chroalians appeared on the view screen, and Devlin watched as the screen flickered and the space elves disappeared from the corridor, leaving a confused-looking security team.

"Open the channel," demanded Holjin. "Report, Cins."

"There's no one here, Captain." Cins, the lead security officer stared around, perplexed. "But the door to sector three is sealed and we can't get through from this side."

Holjin turned back to Sihil. "Where have they gone?"

"Can't tell, the internal sensors aren't responding."

Holjin dashed back into his ready room and returned armed.

"Sihil, take Ambassador Taylor into my ready room and stay there until I give the all-clear."

Devlin thought better than arguing, but he had no way of defending himself from heavily armed space elves, and as much as he'd like to be of use, he'd probably just get in the way and put others in danger. Sihil grabbed his arm and marched him into Holjin's ready room, the door closing behind them.

"Computer lockdown ready room one, clearance code. Sihil 82-3." She was over by the bank of monitors and saw one of them had the same view as he had been watching on the bridge.

He came over to stand by her. "Is this a common occurrence?"

She smiled wryly at him. "You seem rather calm over all this."

"I'm not sure there's any other way to react. No point screaming, all that'll do is make me look like I shouldn't be here in the first place. And they're not exactly my first experience of hostile aliens."

"I had heard the Earth had received a few nasty bastards. Were you involved with the Panchian?"

They were the final straw, the reason he'd decided to change track. "Unfortunately so. Earth was housing someone they wanted, and they were under my protection. I couldn't stop them, and I was lucky to escape with my life."

"You can't blame yourself, Devlin. From what I've seen of you, I'm sure you did everything you could."

He knew he had, but he couldn't win them all. "But these aren't them. I'd recognise a Panchian anywhere."

"There's something strange here. It's rare for us to encounter a completely new-to-us species in such a manner. While not all first contact is friendly, I've never been boarded by an unknown."

"That suggests that you've been boarded by a known species."

She chuckled. "Indeed. But for now, we're under special lockdown protocol, so you're safe in here. Nothing's getting through that door."

"Do you expect them to want to? If they want to commandeer the bridge, they don't need to get in here, and they can just wait us out."

Sihil grabbed two guns from the cabinet in the corner. "Are you always so positive or is today special?"

He laughed. "I'm a realist. But I can be upbeat if the situation requires it. I'm not seeing the reason at the moment as we'll be locked behind a door where several hostile aliens are on the other side."

"No, on the other side is the bridge crew, no hostiles yet. And unless they can get through the security there's unlikely to be."

"Then why did we fall back to here?" He thought it was a reasonable question.

"The captain will not want to be the one in charge if the new Earth ambassador gets injured. Don't forget, there's the fact he's not bedded you yet." She winked at him. "If you want this level of protection to continue, you're best off playing hard to get."

"I have no intention of sleeping with the captain."

She looked at him carefully. "Why not? He's attractive enough, unless you don't go for men."

"Just because I fancy men, doesn't mean I fancy all men. If you think he's so good-looking, you sleep with him."

"I already did, years ago, and he's pretty decent. You don't know what you're missing. Chroalian men will be different to humans. Aren't you even slightly curious?"

He wasn't sure how the conversation had veered in this direction; he barely knew her, and she was trying to get him to shag the captain. "Where I come from people don't ask relative strangers about their sex lives."

"Really? Well, you're on a Chroalian ship now, so if I were you, I'd get used to it. Besides, we're not strangers, not now we're trapped together in this room. Could be more embarrassing—I could be the one wanting to see what sex was like with a human."

She waggled her eyebrows at him, and he couldn't help but laugh. "Even if we weren't in a life-threatening situation, I'm afraid I'd have to respectfully turn you down."

"Oh, you break my heart. But I have to ask: is it because I'm a Chroalian or because I'm a woman?"

"I've no problem with you being a Chroalian."

"Then why not the good captain?"

"If I wanted to get to know a Chroalian, then I think I have plenty of other options. I'd prefer not to be chewed up and spat out, thanks very much." He could hardly say because he was already entangled with a Chroalian, and Holjin's modus operandi seemed like a decent enough excuse for now.

"He does have that sort of reputation, but then he's not the only one on the ship with a racy past. It kinda comes with the territory of being space explorers."

He wasn't sure if she was still joking, but he noticed she was examining the gun she'd collected, and he realised that she was trying to distract him from what was happening elsewhere on the ship.

"I think I'm too old for those games. I'd like to see the universe with someone special by my side. I'm not ruling out that being a Chroalian if the right one was to come along." He didn't think it would hurt to sprinkle a few ideas that would support his and Zal's plan.

"Oh, now that is interesting. Could you possibly already have someone in mind?" She grinned. "Zal Catenmir isn't exactly hard on the eyes."

Devlin hadn't expected her to jump to the right conclusion. "He is very nice."

She handed him one of the guns. "Then we better make sure you get out of here in one piece if you're going to try and win fair Zal. He's been a bit reserved of late, so you've a challenge on your hands to melt him."

The thought of Zal made him realise that he was out there somewhere on the ship, and unlikely behind reinforced doors. "I hope he's safe."

"He'll be fine. The surrounding decks have been sealed off, and the computer hasn't identified him as at risk. He might be a bit concerned about you, but since he'll know you're with the captain he shouldn't worry too much."

He examined the gun he'd been given and it reminded him of something out of a 1990s sci-fi TV series, and vaguely reminiscent of Lego. "I assume this is point-and-shoot?" he asked, holding up the gun.

"Pretty much. I guess you've fired one like that before."

"Ballistic-based, bullets, not lasers." He felt a sort of muscle memory as he held it. "Can't say I was the biggest fan of using them. But I did when I had to, and I suppose that'll be the case now."

"I've used a ballistic weapon, the main difference is the recoil—you'll get less with these." She pointed out a number of features, including an intensity setting. "These are programmed to stun. I'd prefer to take our new friends alive so we can interrogate them to find out who they are and their motivation for coming aboard."

"You don't think they're here to steal the ship?"

She turned to the screen. "They'd have made their way to the bridge by now if they were. They're after something else, but I've no idea what."

"Where are they going?"

"Looks like the cargo bay. They could be as simple as high-tech robbers seeing what we might have on offer."

Something about the way she'd spoke made Devlin suspect she might have a different view but had chosen not to reveal it. He had to remember that while Sihil had been a great companion, she was still a member of the senior crew and wasn't about to tell Devlin everything.

He stared at the screen again. Two of the aliens seemed to be having an argument. "Trouble in paradise."

"I wouldn't call where they are paradise," she said sounding confused.

"Sorry, an Earth colloquialism, means they seem to be arguing with each other. I guess they aren't happy to be here either."

"They might have planned to have been in and out by now, to have gone undetected like their ship."

"But you found their ship."

"Yes, thanks to your suggestion, we recalibrated our scans and picked up an outline of a vessel. It's within teleportation range and the hull shape is a bit strange." She made a wavy pattern with her hand. "What we can't see is how the ship would have been able to get through our precautions; it would take a concerted effort to have done so."

"Unless they knew people who knew how to do it, and they had a reason to help them."

"That infers it was someone from the crew." That, he could see, disturbed her greatly. "There would only be a handful on board who could even think about doing it, and we've got those under close surveillance."

"I'd have thought you'd have wanted anyone with even a suspicion of ill-will off the ship." Somehow it seemed to fly in the face of the way he'd seen Holjin act. "If I were captain, I wouldn't want the risk."

"If proven, then yes. But up until now, there was no evidence to remove someone, and if we were to do so, it would effectively ruin someone's life on a whim. That's not the way we operate as a species, at least not anymore."

"You're better than humans then—we've a long history of making bad decisions quickly. But in my experience, there's usually an outside influence and not just an internal rogue operator."

She eyed him curiously. "What sort of experience made you come to that conclusion?"

"The Ministry is not a universally popular organisation; it is expensive to run and there are high-placed politicians who don't necessarily see the positives of supporting alien settlers. They are happy for us to have been running interference with criminals, but the rest is immaterial." He remembered the days upon days of debriefs that had happened after the event; it still filled him with a wave of tiredness just thinking about it. "Someone tried to sabotage our mission, and we uncovered them before anything of note occurred, but potential risk terrified the higher-ups and a torrent of new protocols were put in place, some of which were counterproductive, in my mind."

She frowned. "Are you suggesting that whoever they are, they have help?"

"Yes, everything points to them not acting alone. They've even masked their appearance so well that, instead of you thinking they are in disguise, your reaction is to believe they are an unknown species. Ask yourself, how likely is that?"

"The chance of us encountering an unknown species in this sector is remote; it's well charted and there have been extensive research missions, meaning the lifeforms are known. We'd even be able to tell you if a type of grass was out of place on some of the planets here."

The monitor flashed on for a few seconds, no longer, but in that time the invaders reappeared and then disappeared. "Computer, are the hostiles still on the ship?"

"Negative."

"Scan the vessel on the port side. Track its course."

"There is no vessel in range," replied the computer.

Devlin knew the Earth didn't have the level of technology of the Chroalians, but surely this was impossible—things and people didn't disappear into thin air. "This doesn't make any sense. Where did they go?"

"I've no idea. How can they vanish without a trace?"

"I assume it's not a dimensional shift?"

She shook her head. "Not unless it is not only a new species, but they also have a way of moving that we've never encountered before. Breaking a number of the laws of physics on the way."

"Which begs the question, were they ever on board?"

She looked stymied by his response. "Something to raise at the debrief."

The door slid open and Holjin reappeared, his stance still coiled, ready for action. Nothing of his potential lover persona was present for now. "Sihil, if you wouldn't mind escorting Ambassador Taylor back to his cabin, then report straight back."

"Yes, sir."

Holjin was clearly rattled and for now Devlin thought it best just to follow Sihil out. He'd talk to Zal later, but he couldn't shake the feeling there was so much more here than an opportunistic boarding party.

Chapter Seven

The ship's computer was in lockdown, standard protocol during tactical manoeuvres. The amber emergency lights and the accompanying worries were giving Zal a headache. Zal tapped frantically at the screen. "Computer, where is Ambassador Taylor?"

"Insufficient clearance for that information."

He knew that, but he had to try. There was no point in having security relays if they were easy to circumnavigate. They were to keep high-priority individuals safe and to stop someone using the computer to locate them if they were boarded. But it meant that Zal had no way of knowing where Devlin was, or if he had been caught up in whatever the emergency was. If he'd been with the captain, there was a good chance he could have been in the wrong place at the wrong time.

He had to stop thinking like this, his brain racing with all the ridiculous possibilities. Several deep breaths later, Zal tried the computer again. "Put me through to Ambassador Scrillia."

The emergency clearance between him and his parents was standard, the familial tie the justification, which he couldn't use for Devlin, not yet anyway.

"Zal?" his mum answered. "Are you okay?"

"I don't know where Devlin is, Mum. I'm scared he's hurt somewhere, or hiding on his own."

The lighting changed hue, a sign that the emergency was coming to an end. "Darling, everything will be okay. You know he was with the captain, and Holjin would not have let anything happen to him. You just need to be patient."

He knew he needed to clear the channel, to avoid unnecessary communication even now as things were improving. "I'm trying. Speak to you later."

Somehow he'd managed to calm himself to a quiet panic. It wouldn't be long now until normal conditions were resumed and he would be able to locate Devlin. Now was not the time to wander off; he should stay put and wait. He sat cross-legged on Devlin's bed, the alarms not so loud in here and the lights almost normal, although that didn't help his headache. He wished he'd brought his tablet with him—that way he could have distracted himself with the reports he'd been reading.

The low hissing noise made him look up to see the door to Devlin's cabin slide open. Devlin wandered in as if he didn't have a care in the universe. "Zal!" he called, smiling. "What are you doing in here? I was going to change and come and find you."

Zal tried to keep his temper even, counting to twenty in at least three languages. Devlin seemed oblivious to his concern and was slipping off his suit jacket, and humming softly. "Where have you been?"

"I was with Holjin. He was giving me a tour of the ship and its mission. We were in his ready room when the aliens boarded, and I holed up in there." Devlin's brow furrowed. "Is there something wrong?"

"There was a general alert, and I didn't know where you were. I was worried sick."

"Oh, Zal, I'm sorry. I thought you'd know where I was." Devlin clambered onto the bed and pulled Zal into his arms. Zal went willingly and clung to the front of Devlin's shirt. "The captain assigned Sihil to keep me safe, and then she escorted me back."

"Sihil? Really? But she's second in command." He should have trusted Holjin to ensure Devlin's safety; he was a capable captain, but Zal had been blinded by his own insecurities.

"I was in good hands. Even gave me a quick lesson on the standard-issue firearms while we were waiting." Devlin pulled back a little and kissed him. "I didn't realise you thought I was in danger. I thought you'd know where I'd be."

"I should have realised you weren't in danger, not when Holjin was there. He may be many things, but he looks after his crew."

"He's a decent man. Thinks a lot of himself, but I get the sense it's mostly deserved." Devlin stroked his hair. "I must say, I was expecting worse based on your reaction to him. Maybe there's something you want to tell me that's causing your reaction? You don't have to, but I get the sense something's been bothering you."

Zal moved so he sat in front of Devlin. Now was as good a time as any to have this discussion, and from the way Devlin had said it, Zal could tell he already had some knowledge. "Let's put it this way, I wasn't immune to Holjin's charms. But it didn't happen after I came back from Earth; it was not long after I first came to join my parents."

Devlin took his hand. "Even if it had, we weren't together, and I wouldn't have thought any worse of you. But you still seem a bit preoccupied with what happened."

"Not in the way you're probably thinking. It was one night, and I have no interest in repeating it."

Devlin bit his lip. "Then what's the issue?"

"Holjin wants you."

"Well, he can't have me."

Zal leant forwards and stroked Devlin's cheek. "I know. I was being an idiot. I've been thinking, and I subconsciously superimposed what I did when I first left Chroalia onto how you might want to behave now you've left Earth. I was what you might call free-spirited."

"Is that another way of saying you had sex with a lot of people when you left home, and you thought I might want to do the same?"

Put like that it made Zal sound even more of an arsehole. "You left Earth so we could be together, I know that you're not going to do anything to jeopardise that. I don't know why I'm trying to self-sabotage the best thing that's ever happened to me."

"It's fine, Zal. Don't beat yourself up over it. I might get an offer, but I've only got eyes for you." He squeezed Zal's hand. "Just how free-spirited were you? Actually, you don't have to tell me, your past is your own, and who you had sex with before isn't any of my business. Unless you're telling me you're planning to start up again."

Devlin's smile was tight. While Zal was aiming for light-hearted, he needed to make sure that Devlin knew that he wasn't interested in anyone else either. "No! Honestly, Devlin. I enjoyed the freedom at the time, and it was what I needed at that point in my life, but these days, I only want you."

"Then we're fine. I would ask a small favour though, I know it's a large universe, but if I'm going to end up meeting someone from your past, I'd rather know upfront. Just so I can do the smug 'I know, but he's mine now' routine, rather than the awkward 'I didn't know' gawping."

It was the open door he needed to explain about Brilli and Appla. "There is someone else you should know about, and our sexual involvement ended ages ago. But we are still close friends, best friends even, although our relationship might sound a bit complicated."

"I'm not someone to judge, Zal. Just tell me."

"It's Commander Brilli, the Chief Communications Officer. We were friends who sometimes had sex with each other, but never anything deeper than that. Then he met his partner, now bond-mate, Appla."

"Ah, I see. Well, I guess it might be uncomfortable for her and you if their involvement put a stop to the fun."

"Appla's species is non-binary, they don't refer to themselves by gendered pronouns. And we were sort of all involved; it worked well up to a point. Brilli and Appla were a constant couple, and I'd join in every so often when the mood took us, nothing regular or involving a commitment as lovers."

Devlin didn't let go of his hand, but Zal could tell he was trying to process what he was saying. It had taken long enough for him to truly understand. They'd been a safe harbour, somewhere to retreat when he needed to have some downtime.

"Sounds like it might have developed into more. Although I didn't realise your tastes included sharing partners." His gaze dropped and he stared at their hands, then looked up again. "How did it end?"

It was a simple question, with no insinuation behind it as far as Zal could tell. Devlin simply wanted to know. "There wasn't anything to end, as such, we were never an official triad. We fooled about when we were in the same location but that wasn't so often, and then I started dating Telgan. When I'm committed to a partner I prefer to be monogamous, and then they got bonded."

"What stopped you from continuing where you left off once you were in the same location as them again and were no longer dating Telgan?"

"None of us wanted to. We decided 'friends only' was much better for us."

Devlin smiled. "Thank you for telling me. I can't say I've had friends like that."

"They're two of my best friends. I'm very close to them, and they are important to me, but not in the way you're important to me."

"I should hope not, or this would be a very different conversation."

Brilli and Appla were important to him, and he wanted them to know how wonderful Devlin was. "I want you to meet them as my friends, not as colleagues. Maybe as a double date."

"I can imagine it might be a bit awkward, but I promise I won't deliberately do anything that would cause problems between you and your friends."

Zal sighed happily as Devlin brushed his lips against his. He didn't know how he'd got so lucky to have Devlin in his life. He wanted Devlin to meet his friends, and he was sure Brilli and Appla would love Devlin. He'd met Brilli, but Appla was a bit more excitable. "I told them about you when I returned. That I loved you and felt I'd left a piece of me behind."

"I'm glad you had someone you could talk to. I wouldn't be

quite so understanding if I thought anything was still going on." Devlin raised an eyebrow. "Your past is your past, but if we're going to have a future, you need to know I'm not the type to share."

"Same for me, Devlin." He pounced and knocked Devlin backwards. "I think we should remind each other exactly who we belong to."

He landed on top of Devlin and claimed a deep kiss, one he'd been desperate to give through the whole time he was worried that Devlin was hurt and injured somewhere without him. Zal needed to convey his love and relief through his kisses, only breaking the kiss to get Devlin out of his clothes. There had to be a way to get Devlin to wear fewer layers as, despite loving how he looked and the sensation being somewhat akin to unravelling a beautifully wrapped gift, what Zal really wanted right now was a naked Devlin so he could suck his cock.

Devlin, thankfully, was on the same page as he was, peeling away his clothes to reveal the soft skin and fuzzy hair that Zal couldn't wait to get his hands on. He had an overbearing need to be inside Devlin, to feel the difference in their temperatures, to be as physically close as possible. The sickness in his stomach that he'd felt when he'd not known where Devlin was had been replaced with an overwhelming urge to be close.

Zal grabbed the lube from the drawer near the bed and watched, his mouth going dry, as Devlin positioned himself flat on his back, naked, legs wide and waiting. He didn't dawdle but slicked up his fingers and slid them into Devlin. This wasn't a moment for slow, considered lovemaking. He wanted quick and deep, reconnecting and claiming Devlin and losing himself to this man.

Devlin was so responsive. They shared filthy, open-mouthed kisses as Zal prepared him. Zal withdrew his fingers, added more lube to his cock, and claimed Devlin in one slow thrust. There was nothing better than being with Devlin. He'd had plenty of lovers in his time, but no one came close to what he felt with him. He began to rock his hips, Devlin's body heat amazing, the extra degrees, coupled with the pressure from his walls, made Zal's scales sing as he set the pace.

He lost himself in the rhythm, Devlin clinging onto him and muttering a string of expressions his translator had no hope of keeping up with. Zal knew they were both close, so he wrapped his hand around Devlin's cock to bring him over the edge, and Devlin came with a shout, the ripples of his orgasm pulling Zal into his own release. He cried out, emptying himself into Devlin.

The universe stood still for a moment and, as his brain rebooted, he slid out of Devlin and claimed another kiss before landing on his side and cuddling in close.

Zal grinned so much his cheeks hurt. He ran his tail across Devlin's stomach. "Well, I'm convinced. We can never split up. You've ruined me for anyone else."

"I think we'll have to do that as a regular event just to make sure neither of us forgets."

Zal snuggled closer. "I don't know what I'd have done if

something had happened to you."

"From what Sihil told me, I was probably in the safest part of the ship. It was pretty exciting, but it was really strange the way they just disappeared."

"I haven't seen any notification of an official briefing. We were just told there'd been a boarding party, and it was being contained. It's pretty standard for the sort of communications the senior crew would put out, and as more reliable information becomes available it gets disseminated. Did you see who it was?" Now his worries for Devlin had been dealt with, his curiosity was back. Eventually he'd be told, but the rumour mill had a penchant for over-exaggeration, and the false whispers would be rife until the captain said something more substantial.

"According to Sihil, they were an unknown species. Although it seemed to me it could have all been an elaborate ruse. Think about it, an unidentified being appears, wanders around a bit, and then—poof—gone."

Zal thought Devlin had a point. "I'll probably be called in to review the footage to see if there were any features that might identify them in some way. Everyone leaves some sort of trace, no matter how small. A soil sample from a boot and few flakes of skin left behind, I can get something off the tiniest fragment."

Devlin made a soft humming noise, the one that told Zal he was contemplating something. "You're going to think me mad, but I'm not convinced they were really here."

"Are you suggesting they were some sort of projection? That

the scans were fooled?"

"I'm not sure what I'm suggesting, and I could be hugely off the mark, but it would be easier to trick the camera and sensors than disappear into nothing. I've seen aliens be able to perform deflection and illusions."

Zal was constantly amazed by Devlin; he was so smart, and Zal was guilty of forgetting that just because Devlin was human, and in theory a less advanced species, didn't mean he wasn't a brilliant man. "Let's see if any samples turn up and, if there's nothing, then that would add credence to your theory."

Devlin squeezed him. "I wanted adventure, and I certainly got it."

Chapter Eight

The morning session with Scrillia was far less arduous than the day before, and Devlin left with the plan to spend some time on his language lessons and reading for their upcoming planetary visit. Zal had been called to a meeting by his boss but had sent him a message to meet to have lunch together, and Devlin was happy to pass the time in the public areas rather than shut himself away in his cabin, so he claimed a table in the mess. He was ploughing through the details of Xoros, and its primary species, who were marginally more advanced than humans had been when they had first started space travel, when he was interrupted as someone dropped into the seat opposite.

For a brief moment, he thought it was Zal, due to the flash of orange hair, but it wasn't. Instead, a young female Chroalian sat grinning at him. "I saw you sitting here all on your own, and I thought, 'There is a man who could do with some company.'"

She was as forthright as Zal. "I suppose I am here to meet new people."

"The name's Rila. I'm an ensign in engineering. And I like to think I'm one of the friendly ones."

He suspected she might be one of the ensigns Zal had mentioned who were betting between themselves on who could bed the most aliens on their current rotation. It was sort of flattering, although he didn't much like being thought of as a trophy to be won. "I've not met any unfriendly ones here yet."

"Some of us are more friendly than others," she said with a wink. Rila leant forwards and he noticed that she'd pulled down the front of her overalls so that her impressive cleavage and low-cut tank top with her scales in a pretty pattern across her collarbones were on display. "I've just come off duty, so I've plenty of time to be even friendlier. If you'd like to spend some time together, we can see how well we could get on."

He'd seen for himself that Chroalians were far more open when it came to sex and physicality in general when compared to humans—well, most humans like him—and he wondered if this was what Zal had been like when he was younger. Zal's concerns that he thought Devlin might mind about his past had been endearing, although it did go to show they had much to learn about each other. Devlin wasn't the type to judge on past life activities but he also wasn't the type to share, and he'd been glad Zal was on the same page regarding monogamy after their chat about Brilli and Appla.

"That is a very kind offer, but I have to get ready for our visit to Xoros. It will be my first visit to an alien planet and I want to be prepared. Don't want to mess up my new assignment."

She licked her lips. "One way of preparing yourself is practising with a friendly alien. I wouldn't mind being your first alien encounter."

"You're a bit late for that, I'm afraid. My role at the Ministry back on Earth meant I got to meet all sorts of wonderful people from various sectors of the universe."

Her nostrils flared, and her eyes were turning purple. "But maybe not Chroalian."

"It is a generous offer, but I'm going to have to politely refuse."

"Why? Where's your spirit of adventure?"

"It is no reflection on you, just that I tend to appreciate the male form."

"Oh." She smirked and her tail shimmied. "Well, at least I can retain my ego. I was beginning to think I was losing my touch. I'd better leave you to it, but let's have a drink sometime. I can share notes on crew members who are open to fun with boys and girls."

Rila slinked away, her tail waving, and he saw her stop to whisper something to a couple of young men. He suspected his peace would not last long. Zal had warned him to expect the attention, but he'd put that down to Zal's own attraction towards him. But it appeared he was wrong as the young man who sat down so brazenly in front of him looked like he wanted to eat him alive. His eyes were already bright purple, and his black hair made his skin impossibly pale, almost ethereal or fae-like. With his looks and build, Devlin thought there would be fashion designers back on Earth willing to fight to the death to dress him in their latest collections.

"Rila says you like to fuck men. I would very much like to volunteer."

"Ensign Karan," barked a voice that made both Karan and Devlin jump in their seats. Devlin turned to see Sihil standing with her arms crossed over her chest. "This is not a dance club or a bar, so you will not treat the mess as a playground for you to pick up sexual partners."

Karan shot to his feet. "Sorry, Commander."

"It's not me you should be apologising to." Her gaze darted to Devlin. "I know you and your little friends have your games, but Ambassador Taylor is off-limits. Understand?"

"Yes, Commander."

"Now get out of my sight before I have you rostered on for a double shift cleaning the waste outlets."

"Apologies, Ambassador. I meant no disrespect." He darted away and Sihil chuckled.

"I do hope I interpreted your expression correctly, and I haven't—What do you call it?—chock docked you."

He laughed. "It's cock blocked, and no, I'm more than happy to be rescued. Mind you, it's not every day I get hit on by two attractive aliens in the space of five minutes."

"It's fine if you want that, but some of our young studs need a kick up the tail. If you don't want to be targeted so obviously, I suggest you avoid the change of shift as I fear you've probably gone up in the most-wanted stakes."

"Zal did say there was some sort of betting pool."

"It's mostly harmless, but they need to be reminded that there are boundaries and they shouldn't overstep them. Not all species are as open as Chroalians."

He'd hoped Zal would be here by now, but it looked like he'd be better off heading to his cabin. "I was planning to have lunch with Zal, but I guess something came up. Best head to higher ground to avoid the hunting pack."

"I doubt he'll be free for a while. He's been pulled into the investigation on the boarding party."

That'd explain it, and he suspected Zal hadn't been given the opportunity to get a message to him. "I'll go back to my cabin for a while. It's a bit too early for lunch."

"How about you come with me? I promised the captain I'd give you a firearms and hand-to-hand combat lesson."

He glanced down at the suit he was wearing. "I'm not exactly dressed for action."

"There'll be spare kit in the gym. Come on."

With no real reason to turn her down, he followed her to the lift, and he realised they were heading to the bowels of the ship on the same levels as the cargo bay, and he hadn't been there before.

The lift opened into a large hangar, and Sihil guided him away from the hustle and bustle of a busy cargo bay, where what he assumed were maintenance crews looked to be working on several land vehicles, towards a set of double doors.

"Firing range or hand-to-hand fighting first?" she asked.

He'd never been the most dedicated to an exercise routine, but he did think he could do with expending some energy. "I say let's see you knock me on my arse first. I sense you might enjoy it."

The door slid open to reveal a corridor. "Locker rooms are that way. You'll find workout clothes on the right. No need for shoes."

Devlin did as instructed, finding piles of soft jogging bottoms, and T-shirts where Sihil had said they would be. He chuckled as he realised all the joggers had a tail hole, but a few minutes later he was stowing his things in a locker and following the signs to the workout area. He found Sihil tapping a panel outside a door and dressed in a similar set of clothes to his own. "This one's free. Don't worry I won't do too much damage to start with."

"Go easy on me, I'm not a complete novice but it's been a while."

She smirked. He was so fucked.

From the look of her in the simple dark blue workout clothes, she could probably snap him in two. She was lean and her muscle mass intimidating, and that was just her biceps.

"Come at me. I want to see what you've got, and then we'll see how you defend."

He was beginning to regret this idea, but he wasn't going to back out as he suspected she'd enjoy teasing him even more if he begged off. Also, he liked her, and the idea that he had made a new friend independent of Zal meant he wasn't going to waste the opportunity.

Falling back to his training, he went for her legs, going in low to take her out, but she was too quick for him, and moments later he found himself on his back staring at the ceiling. She offered him her hand to help him up, which he accepted. "Nice idea, but obvious. If your attacker's unbalanced or on the run, taking their legs is a great idea, but I was well centred and expecting you."

He pounced, grabbed her arm behind her back and forced her to her knees. She swore loudly, twisted in his grip and once again he was flat on his back. "Impressive. Not many can say they've got the drop on me. I think a few sessions and you'll be lucky not to be on security rotation with moves like that."

"No chance," he said, getting to his feet. "As far as I'm concerned, you're meant to be providing me with a security detail. I'm just there to look cute in a suit."

"Oh don't worry, pretty prince, no one's gonna be allowed to ruffle your feathers. Not without an express invite."

Devlin enjoyed the session—he got a decent workout and Sihil was generous with her praise and her guidance. He'd not been lying when he'd said he was rusty, but he now felt much more confident and he reckoned he could give any wannabe attacker a run for their money.

She was relentless though, and he'd as much time on his back with Sihil as he did Zal, although for very different reasons.

"Truce," he croaked out as she sat astride him, her arm across his throat.

"Well, this wasn't what I had in mind when you said you were going to spend time preparing for Xoros." Devlin saw Zal staring at the edge of the mat, looking like he was trying not to laugh, his eyes a lime green, a colour he'd not seen before. "Looks fun!"

Sihil grinned and got off Devlin. "Hey, Zal. I didn't think you'd be allowed out of the lab for a while."

"I've left a load of samples running," he said. "I was hoping if Devlin had finished having his arse kicked, he might like lunch."

Sihil let Zal pull her to her feet. "The captain has asked that the ambassador be given some self-defence classes."

"Yeah, I saw that on the list, but didn't know it was now." Devlin saw Zal wink at her. "I would just like to be informed of Devlin's activities so I can best support him. There is a log set up to make that easier. And I might be available to join in."

Devlin wasn't sure if Zal was genuinely okay with finding him rolling on the floor with Sihil or masking it well. "I'm guessing after yesterday, Zal might be a little concerned about my whereabouts. He didn't know I was locked in the captain's ready room."

She sauntered past Zal, calling back as she went to the changing room. "He's perfectly safe. And in case you're available, I'd like him to come to me at the same time tomorrow—firearms training this time. I've a handful of others coming along if you're interested."

Left alone, Devlin turned to Zal. "Is everything all right?"

"Next time I find you on your back with a woman straddling you, I'll be wanting to join in." Zal grinned. "She is kinda hot."

He was pretty sure Zal was joking, but he thought a little reassurance wouldn't hurt. "You know I've no interest in Sihil. I think she might become a friend if I'm lucky."

Zal grinned. "Yeah, she's great. And good for you to get to know more people."

"I was being hit on by over-eager ensigns and she rescued me. Some of them are extremely forward."

"Someone hit you?" asked Zal, scandalised.

Now was not the best time for a misunderstanding. "No, hit on. As in, they were offering to have sex with me."

"I did try and warn you about what they were like. I know because I was exactly the same at their age. But they're even worse because they are surrounded by equally horny individuals every day, and so when someone new comes along, you're an obvious target. Who was it?"

"Rila and Karan."

Zal let out a low whistle. "You've attracted a fine pair there. But then, you're super sexy, so I'm gonna have to up my game to make sure you remember I'm your favourite Chroalian."

Again Zal didn't seem overly concerned, and in fact, he didn't seem bothered at all, and considering how he'd acted over Holjin, it surprised Devlin. "Let me grab a shower, and then we can go get lunch. I'm dying to hear about the samples you're running."

Chapter Nine

Zal prodded his lunch, which they'd collected from the mess but had taken to Zal's cabin. He'd already been in a bit of a strange mood after the security breach investigation had dragged him in, and they had him looking at things that weren't there. Frustrating wasn't a strong enough word for it. But then he'd gone in search of Devlin and had been surprised when the computer had directed him to Workout Hall Three. Finding Sihil sitting astride Devlin had caused a bolt of unwarranted fiery jealousy, but he'd been hit with a realisation he was being a giant idiot, and it was actually funny that Devlin thought he had any chance against Sihil in a fistfight. He knew it had been completely innocent—Sihil was meant to be giving Devlin hand-to-hand combat training, and Devlin had no interest in any woman. Putting it all into perspective meant he hadn't been overly bothered when he'd heard two members of the crew had already tried their luck earlier. Devlin was free game at the moment in the eyes of others, but he knew better, and Devlin had proved he could be trusted by sending them away and telling Zal what had happened.

"Zal, is there something wrong?" Devlin asked, reaching out to stroke the back of Zal's hand. "If it's about Sihil, there's nothing going on. As I said, I think she might be nice to have as a friend."

He must have been too quiet, and the last thing he wanted was for Devlin to think him upset. Devlin needed to have friends other than him—this was a brilliant sign he was adapting well to leaving Earth if he was already thinking Sihil could fill the role of close friend. "Sorry, I zoned out a bit. It's been one of those mornings. I admit that when I first saw you and Sihil together, I was a bit jealous, but I soon untangled my tail. I can't wait for everyone to know you're mine though."

"It won't be for long. I've only been on board a few days. You're coming down to the surface of Xoros, so why don't we try and organise something we could use as a trigger to show when we started dating?"

"Yes, that'll be a good start. But, Devlin…?"

"Yes."

He dropped his gaze to stare at his fingers, something that had been bothering him drifting to the surface, but now might not be the best moment. Part of his unease was his earring, or rather how it was no longer in Devlin's possession. Devlin had asked him to give it back when Zal was ready to give it to him as if they had been a normal couple, but he now wished he'd insisted Devlin kept it. He'd bring it up another time. "Actually, I was thinking that there'll be an official function sooner rather than later on the ship, and you could go as my date." He looked up and smiled. "It can be our first public expression of interest in each other."

"That sounds lovely. Although expression of interest does sound like you're planning some sort of hostile takeover of my person." Devlin chuckled. "Let's face it, we both know there's nothing hostile about that."

Zal loved Devlin's sense of humour, and if he hadn't needed to return to the lab after lunch he'd have had Devlin on his back in a heartbeat. "Remember that thought for this evening. Once I've escaped the lab."

"I was going to ask about that. Can you tell me what's going on? Any news on the investigation?"

There was probably a protocol around disclosing this sort of information, but as no one had told him of its existence, Zal decided he could claim ignorance if challenged about talking to Devlin. "Because there wasn't positive ID made of the species that boarded, I was asked to test around a hundred samples that were taken in various parts of the ship that the aliens were supposedly in."

"Doesn't sound that many to me," Devlin said. "Some of the Ministry investigations we carried out could analyse thousands of samples, taking weeks. I know our tech is less advanced, but I would think there would always be a maximum throughput possible."

"You're right, it's a ridiculously small amount for the area in the zones being investigated. Which should have rang alarm bells with the investigation team to start with. I said this in the briefing and Holjin agreed but said it was what it was." He'd been even more annoyed that a lot of the samples were barely more than bits of dust.

"So they were inconclusive?" asked Devlin.

"They're bizarre. There wasn't anything that shouldn't have already been present on the ship. Even the microscopic fragments of mud I analysed could be traced back to the last planet we used the terrain vehicles on and, as they are being serviced for use on Xoros, it's not surprising that carryover dirt was found."

Devlin made a low humming noise. "Nothing to suggest a new alien species then?"

"No, or visitors from a known species disguising themselves as an unknown species."

He could tell Devlin was working through an idea. He recognised the specific look. "So the idea I floated to you yesterday about these aliens not being there; is it a possibility?"

In real terms, Zal hadn't known Devlin that long, but he considered that he knew him well, and this leap of logic had surprised him yesterday. Still, there had to have been more to his introspection than low sample numbers and non-interpretable results. "I think so. But I should have asked before, how did you come to think it?"

Devlin smirked. "Are you asking how did the apeman come

to think this when the Chroalians didn't?"

Zal winced. "I didn't mean it like that."

"I know, but your commanding officers will. Anyway, to start with, the scans didn't pick up their ship, and when they were reconfigured, it came across as a shadow. Which to me didn't prove there was anything there."

"What do you mean?"

Devlin leant back in his chair. "What was it a shadow of? Sihil said it had a strange-shaped hull, but couldn't it just have been a distorted shadow of the *Endeavour*?"

"I suppose so, but I would have thought the scans would have been calibrated to prevent that sort of thing, and the ship's sensors did pick up beings on the ship that weren't meant to be there."

"Did they? Or were they projections of a bunch of figures walking down a corridor? No one engaged them, and when the security team turned up they'd gone, so the only sightings were on the monitors."

Devlin was certainly thinking around corners, but he wasn't wrong. "That suggests something tricked our internal sensors into thinking we were being boarded. Why do that?"

"I dunno. I did ask if it could be explained by a species capable of dimensional shifting. None of the species I've met can do that in the way we saw, as if the being had stepped into a different dimension, but then there's more out there I don't know than do know."

Zal shook his head. "No, you're right, there's no one I know who can do that in the sense they'd be able to disappear without trace and not leave behind any evidence they were there in the first place. Most leave an energy signal behind, if not body parts."

"Then if you put that with the sample weirdness and the fact they disappeared into thin air, then an obvious possibility is they were never here in the first place."

"And you said you'd brought this idea to Sihil?"

"Yes, she said it would be a matter for the briefing, but from your reaction nothing's been said."

All that meant was nothing had been said while Zal was present. He wouldn't have been invited to the initial discussion of Holjin's senior team. "I've got to present my findings so far after the next cycle of samples has finished. Why don't you come with me and ask to put forward your hypothesis?"

"Would that be allowed?"

"The captain can always send you away, but from what I've seen he's stuck for ideas, and if he had discounted yours already it would be an ideal time to remind him of it again."

*

Devlin had a healthy respect for being nervous, which meant he could recognise it in others. After lunch, Zal had returned to his lab, but as promised had collected him en route to the meeting to provide an update. Holjin didn't look particularly happy to see him.

"Ambassador Taylor, I wasn't aware you were invited."

Sihil raised an eyebrow as Zal answered, "I believe the ambassador can offer us a unique insight. I invited him to attend. Given the situation, I don't think we can afford to overlook an additional perspective here."

"Actually, I agree," said Sihil. "I was in the ready room during the incident and Ambassador Taylor was the one who suggested the scans' recalibration."

Devlin followed Zal's lead and sat at the table with several of the senior crew. "It wasn't the only thing I suggested."

Holjin cleared his throat. "Right, let's get started. Lieutenant Catenmir, an overview of your results please."

Devlin noticed the use of rank and titles and suspected it was deliberate to avoid informality during a serious discussion. Zal brought up a presentation on the holographic projector. "I received the sample set this morning and have performed the full gamut of tests available on board for the type of samples there were. To be brutally honest, the sample size was very low, given the investigation area and type of incursion. I wasn't able to isolate any genetic material belonging to individuals not identified as already being on the ship, the slight traces of mud were linked to the vehicles in the cargo bay, and there was nothing out of the ordinary in the air samples collected."

The slides showed a collection of charts and figures that amounted to diddly-squat, not the scientific conclusion, but the gist of Zal's research.

"So what does that mean?" asked Holjin.

"There is no evidence, at least from the samples tested, that there was anyone on board the *Endeavour* who shouldn't have been." Zal glanced at Devlin. "It supports the hypothesis I know was already put forward by Ambassador Taylor, so I'll repeat it. Were we really boarded, or just made to think we were?"

"I did report this as a possibility as part of the senior team brief," said Sihil. "And now looking at the additional evidence from Lieutenant Catenmir and the information from the scans, I would think it the most logical scenario."

"The hypothesis raises the same question now as it did then," Holjin said with a sigh. "Who would do that, and what possible motive would they have to do so?"

"I can think of several," Devlin said, not wanting to overstep, but the expressions worn around the table made him think his intervention would be welcomed.

"Please do enlighten us, Ambassador," Holjin drawled, although there was no real snideness behind it.

"One plausible reason is to test your systems, to find the weak links where the defence is the most vulnerable. This could be either to help, as identifying the gaps to prevent an attack in the future, or to exploit the system and control the ship."

Holjin seemed to be considering the points. "It's a possibility, and the reasons behind it are valid. We shouldn't discount the idea of malevolent species that are just there to cause chaos; they could simply be playing with us."

"I guess if you can identify who might be interested in either helping our security or compromising it, then you'd have a good chance of preventing a future attack," Devlin said. It seemed pretty obvious to him, but in his previous role he'd learnt what he thought was obvious wasn't always so to other people.

"Sounds like a starting point. I'm not aware of anyone offering a service that would challenge a ship's security."

Devlin wondered if that was true. This wasn't a new ruse, and on Earth the ruse happened all the time. He would have bet his own legs that there would have been specialists that either offered the service or had been caught trying to wreak havoc and then been forced to help or face punishment. "Are you sure? On Earth, the financial sector and several governments have employed security services to check for weak points for years."

Holjin's nostrils flared, and his eyes flashed dark blue, almost black. "I'm not in the habit of withholding information, Ambassador Taylor. If I was aware and had the clearance to share, I would have said so."

Sihil came to his rescue. "I'll instigate a database sweep, see if there's anything on record relating to those possibilities and see where it leads us. There may be historical examples, back to when Chroalia was in a similar developmental phase to Earth."

Devlin wasn't convinced, nor did he like the insinuation it was only Earth's lack of maturity that meant it would be a possibility.

"Very well. I suggest we reconvene at the start of the next shift rotation." Holjin closed down the projector. "Ambassador

Taylor, if you would remain for a moment. I'd like to discuss the Xoros visit."

"Is there anything I should be aware of, as the ambassador's liaison?" Zal asked, clearly not wanting to leave Devlin with Holjin.

"I just wanted to impart Devlin with the benefit of my experience; nothing for you to worry about." He flashed Zal a smile. "I'll send him back safe and sound, don't worry."

Zal rolled his eyes, but Devlin knew he had no real reason to object, so he followed the others out. Devlin suspected Holjin didn't like the way he had questioned him. He was on his ship by his grace, and it wouldn't do him any good in the long run to antagonise him. "Captain, I apologise if I stepped out of line."

"I'm not the sort of man who needs to be surrounded by yes-men, but I would appreciate it if, in the future, you might challenge me in such a way, that you do so in private."

"Of course. I do hope this won't impact our working relationship. I also recognise I turned up to your meeting without permission, which I apologise for."

Holjin laughed. "No need. Your insights have been extremely helpful, and I can see why you were appointed as ambassador. I think you being on board will bring a great benefit to the crew."

Devlin stood, preparing to leave. "I'd like to think so."

"Now to the reason I asked you to stay." Holjin took a few steps closer. "We were rudely interrupted last time we talked, and I wanted to find a way to make up for that."

Holjin's change of demeanour would make a less experienced man's head spin, but Devlin had spent years in the British civil service and had rarely started a project without it changing direction three times. "And now it's my turn to say it's not necessary."

"I insist."

He stepped away before Holjin could move closer. "You said you didn't like yes-men so here's me saying, very clearly, no."

"No?" He smirked, and Devlin guessed Holjin's charm worked on most of the people he tried it on.

"No. Now, if you'll excuse me, I still have a lot to get prepared for our visit to Xoros."

He left, hearing Holjin's soft chuckle as the door slid shut. He had a sneaking suspicion that Holjin's pursuit of him was far from over and, with Zal already jealous, their public declaration couldn't come soon enough.

Zal was waiting for him outside. "What did he want?"

They'd talked about Holjin before, but the conversation had been about what had happened between him and Zal. "He wanted to carry on the conversation we had in his ready room before we were boarded."

"What was that?"

"I'm sure I don't need to spell it out. But I wasn't interested then, and I'm not interested now."

"I'm sorry, Devlin. The captain's a blind spot of mine. I'm trying. I really am."

Devlin was surprised that Holjin was still a sore point, but then Zal was only flesh and blood. At least his jealousy was limited, as they'd have been in serious trouble if he reacted over everyone who shot him a lascivious look on board.

Chapter Ten

G iven he'd only left Earth three days ago, life had been more eventful than Devlin had been expecting, not that he thought life would be dull travelling on a spaceship. Tomorrow he would be heading to the surface of a new planet, which would have been exciting enough on its own, without the added drama of the *Endeavour* seemingly having been fake boarded. He'd decided those details weren't going to go in his first report back to Earth, but then he was waiting to hear from the communications team when the secure channel he could use would be ready.

Sihil was waiting for him as he left his cabin. "Ready to be equipped for deadly force?" she asked with a smile.

"I thought you preferred to stun first and ask questions later."

"True, and there are certain members of this crew, that if

they don't stop acting like a pizzy diggle waxel, I will do just that."

"Pizzy diggle waxel—I think there's no direct translation but I get the gist. Dare I ask who?"

"Let's just say, if certain ensigns don't want to be assigned cleaning drains for a long stint they should stop proclaiming the naughty things they want to do to you with their tails."

"Oh." Devlin had hoped they'd got the message. "Zal did say they could be very determined."

"He was there when I put a stop to it."

"He was?"

She winked at him. "You're blushing. Aww, Devlin, do you have a crush on your liaison? Zal was joking with a couple of the ensigns that their plans to entice you into a three-way needed to be more robust as an ambassador of your calibre wouldn't be an easy conquest. Kinda sweet really."

It didn't sound sweet, more like Zal might be encouraging the ensigns rather than putting them off, and he wondered if he was overcompensating for his reactions over Holjin. Devlin would have liked Zal to have been a bit annoyed, nothing major but enough to maybe tell the ensigns to pipe down.

He'd only seen Zal briefly after he'd woken up. Zal had been in a grumpy mood after having been called to his lab, so while he hadn't heard anything, he wouldn't have wanted to be on the receiving end of Zal's bad humour, but it sounded like he'd shaken it off if he'd been able to joke around with ensigns. "At least you were there to defend my honour."

She patted his shoulder. "You don't need me for that. But seriously, if you are thinking of starting something with Zal, just a word of advice. I can understand having someone to confide in is important, and he is a friendly face since you'd met before, but don't let him pressurise you into anything."

Devlin thought it nice that she cared, but she didn't know Zal well if she thought he was capable of coercion. "He wouldn't, but there's a definite mutual interest."

She winked at him. "Fair enough. It's my job to notice these sorts of things, when maybe others wouldn't, but if you don't want it to be ship-wide gossip that Catenmir wants to be on the list of many Chroalians who'd like the chance to show you their scales, he probably shouldn't be joking around in the mess with the ensigns who are."

"I'll have a word." He wasn't sure exactly what he'd say, as demanding to know why his boyfriend wasn't being a jealous arse sounded like a wankerish thing to do.

"Good. Anyway, I also thought it might be nice for you to meet a couple of people in a similar situation, in the sense that they're not Chroalians either. I'm sure Zal will have something scheduled for the better-connected individuals, but I promised to give some firearms training to two others who are a little lower in the ranks, so I thought it would be nice to combine."

Devlin was more than happy to meet new people, and Zal had designed a schedule based on who Devlin needed to know first, so this was a nice option. "It's a great idea."

"They're both part of a rotation scheme we have between different species as a way of building trust and sharing knowledge. Pilo, who is a medical technician helping Dr Golic, is from Ramaal in the Topol solar systems and the other is Fyma, an Atrachian, a botanist."

"Is she on Zal's team?" He thought he'd heard Zal mention her.

"I think so. Or at least in that wider group. The technical team do switch around, depending on what they discover, to make the most of their resources."

Waiting for them at the firing range, not far from the gym he'd been at the previous day, were two people. Pilo had deep purple skin and was rather stout, making Devlin think of a blueberry, whereas Fyma was willowy and only a few inches shorter than Devlin, with long silver hair and tan skin colour. They both smiled as he approached, and Pilo gave a little wave.

"Hi, guys. This is Devlin. Your fellow non-Chroalian."

Pilo bounced on the balls of his feet. "We've heard a lot about you coming. It must be so exciting."

"Very much so. This is my first time leaving my planet."

"Me too!" Fyma cried. "I was really scared at first but my uncle thought it would be an excellent opportunity, so I decided to give it a chance."

"What about you, Pilo?" Devlin asked.

"I've been on a couple of rotations now, and it's so nice to meet new people."

Sihil clapped her hands together. "I'm sure the three of you will be great friends. Now, let's go shoot things."

*

Devlin had enjoyed his time on the shooting range and had been surprised by how much muscle memory he had from his previous firearms experience. His fellow non-Chroalians were very sweet, although he sensed they were a little in awe of him, given his standing aboard ship and the accuracy of his headshots. Now he was waiting patiently for Communications Officer Senetric to finish setting up a recording station. They were in a little cubby, a small room not much bigger than a couple of telephone boxes from home. Her fingers flew over the screens in a blur, and she bit her lip in concentration, then let out several frustrated growls until she was ready.

"There we go!" she cried in triumph. "Sorry, Ambassador, the array has been a bit sticky. Not sure why and sometimes catching a signal is like chasing a ghost."

She moved to the side and motioned for Devlin to sit next to her. "Now as I understand it, you're sending a written report rather than wanting a video message or a live feed. At least most of the time."

"Yes, the idea is I report back to Earth on a regular basis. I sort of thought it was already set up."

Senetric smiled apologetically. "It was and we used it several times when arranging the diplomatic visit to Earth. The channel's been a bit temperamental, and I'm not sure why, but it should be fine now. Can you confirm the frequency of how often you plan to contact home?"

He thought this had all been settled by the Ministry, but then they weren't the most thorough over certain things. "Every four to five Earth days to begin with, which I think is closer to three of the Chroalian equivalent."

She looked like she was doing the maths in her head. "Sounds about right. I imagine you're still adapting to the longer days."

He had noticed being a bit more tired, but the excitement had carried him through and there were too many new things to learn and experience to worry about a few extra hours of sleep. He might have a different view if he were sharing a bed with Zal as he doubted he'd have got anywhere near as much sleep. "So far so good. Although we'll see what happens on my first trip to the surface of a planet."

She tapped the screen and their faces appeared. "This here," she said, indicating an illuminated red square, "is the upload button. I'm assuming you've a report on your device or in your private files area, but you can write directly—due to the encryption needed you have to use a station as your devices won't have clearance."

He'd assumed something similar. "I understand. I guess there'll be a review done by the ship's computer of anything I've written."

"Yes, again it's for security reasons. Not that we don't trust you, but you might not realise some of the information which is innocuous to Earth could be sensitive to Chroalia."

That, and they had no reason to trust him yet.

"Press the red square to start and again to finish. Then the yellow one next to it is the review for any spoken playback or images, and the blue is the delete. When you're ready to send, double tap the green circle and key in your security pin."

Part of the documents he'd received when he'd left Earth included his pin although up until now he'd not had a reason for it. "Seems straightforward enough."

"It is. Now you're connected. I'll leave you to it, if you need anything just ask the ship's computer to put you through to me. I'll be at my console."

He'd downloaded the transcripts for his daily journal, so he hoped this would be quick and painless. Peering at the screen, he saw a little icon with 'New message' written underneath. He clicked on it and there appeared an image of a woman he recognised from Earth—Marjorie, his admin. He pressed play.

"Devlin, you sod! You could've at least said goodbye... I hope you're getting to bang your alien boy toy after all this, otherwise it'd be a bit shite." She laughed. "But seriously, I asked Horace if I could record a message, and I was quite surprised he said yes. He thought it might be nice for you to have a friendly face from home, though I'm pretty sure you're getting friendly enough out there."

Her grin was positively filthy. "Anyway, I'm going to send you regular messages, and I think you should be able to send them back. You've got to do the proper ones for the Ministry, but I'd love to be the one who hears the good stuff, and I'll keep you in the loop. I thought you'd like to hear how pissed off Peterson is, and that we've not got a new boss yet. Horace is trying to keep us all in line. Well, you've not been gone long, so I will send you a message every week whether you like it or not." She stuck out her tongue and blew a raspberry before ending her message.

He hadn't been gone a week yet, but seeing Marjorie gave him a pang of homesickness. It wasn't as if he wanted to return to Earth, and it was really silly to feel this way. Despite being rattled, he managed to concentrate long enough to upload his various journal entries and edit them into a comprehensive message back to Earth. The Ministry expected him to cover the salient points but couldn't bring himself just yet to reply to Marjorie, so he'd come back later.

Devlin let Senetric know he was done and headed back to his cabin. He didn't want to be on his own and found himself outside of Zal's door. From what he remembered of his schedule, Zal should have been back from the lab if he hadn't had to remain late. The door opened, keyed to Devlin, and he saw Zal sitting at his workstation.

"Devlin? I wasn't expecting you yet. Everything okay?"

"I could do with a cuddle."

Zal got to his feet and came over to Devlin opening his arms and Devlin let himself be pulled into a hug. "What's wrong?"

"Marjorie sent me a message and made me feel a bit homesick. Not really homesick—it just hit me from nowhere."

Zal stroked his hair and Devlin nuzzled into his neck, Zal's scent reassuring, and he held on to him a little tighter. "How about I give you a massage? Get rid of some of the tension and it lets me get you naked."

"Any excuse to get me out of my suit."

"Always, and sex is a great mood lifter."

Chapter Eleven

Devlin re-read his notes. No matter how many times he'd gone over them before, once more would not hurt. He was waiting in the transporter bay, Zal standing next to him, ready to be transferred to the planet. Tractor beams were already transferring the landovers, the all-terrain vehicles the Chroalians used on the surface of a planet for exploration and sample collection.

Holjin was working through a pre-departure check, and Sihil came to join him. She winked at him. "I've been told I need to stick close to you. The captain wants to make sure nothing damages you in any way."

"I told him I was capable of looking after myself."

"I said the same, but you may have noticed he can be a little single-minded on certain topics."

Zal sniggered. "He'll be too busy dealing with Filote if the notes are correct. Holjin won't have time to worry about the rest of us."

Devlin thought Zal was right. Filote was the First Minister of Xoros's central government, and everything he'd read about her said she liked to be the centre of attention and expected visiting dignitaries to show her the level of respect she thought she deserved.

Sihil chuckled. "Maybe he'll be inducted into her harem. I hear she's got quite a collection."

"I think he'd love it. Best not suggest it or we won't see him for the duration of the visit," Zal said, grinning.

Holjin appeared to be finished and was marshalling people into position. "First wave to beam down."

Zal had grumbled, but his complaints hadn't changed the result, so he was in the second wave whereas Devlin, as Earth's Ambassador, would go down in the first. Sihil grabbed Devlin's arm. "Ready? I remember my first time on a new planet, I was so excited. Ultimately, it wasn't the most exciting, more basic training than anything else, but the thrill of being on an alien world is unbeatable."

Zal pursed his lips and frowned. Devlin found his worried expression adorable, but he wouldn't say that to him. "Be careful, Devlin. I won't be long behind you."

Sihil's smirk disappeared as quickly as it arrived. Her knowing what was going on between them wouldn't be a bad thing, since she'd seemed to approve, but he hadn't spoken to Zal about it yet. "Don't worry, Zal. I'll make sure our precious little Devie is okay."

Devlin spluttered at the awful nickname but didn't have the chance to complain as Sihil dragged him onto the hexagon pad of the transporter.

He'd only travelled this way once, and the experience had been painless. He blinked and opened his eyes. He was on his back staring at an orange-hued sky, Holjin and Sihil leaning over him. "Are you all right?"

"Why am I lying low?" He let Holjin pull him to his feet.

"No idea," Sihil said, her expression pinched. "The chief engineer is trying to figure it out. You took several seconds longer than anyone else to reappear."

Dr Golic barged them out of the way, his handheld scanner out. "I want to double-check the readings. The ship's scans say everything's normal, but a local proximity sweep will confirm."

Holjin was taking special care to brush down the back of Devlin's jacket, his new suit would be his Ambassador uniform, at least for now, although Holjin didn't need to pay such close attention to brushing the imaginary dirt off his arse.

"All seems in order," Dr Golic said, but he didn't sound 100 percent convinced. "I'll stay close to Ambassador Taylor for a while, just to make sure."

"I feel fine," he insisted. Although he knew not to dismiss something not going to plan without due consideration.

"Good, let's keep you that way. You humans are hardy

creatures, but it doesn't mean I want to test out how you'd do in extremes," Dr Golic said.

He was far too excited to be on the surface of his first alien planet to worry further. He'd seen pictures and knew the sky would have a slightly orange hue during the day and the terrain lush as they were a species who had a grounding in agriculture. Its industrialisation hadn't changed its basis but instead had made them a highly valuable trading partner. They'd set down in an area of farmland that looked to have been recently cleared by the way the earth still sat in clods. A track had been made through it and, in the distance, Devlin could see the city, but in every other direction arable farmland stretched out as far as the eye could see. The crop looked similar to wheat and the ocean of tall yellow stems reminded him of the American Midwest back on Earth. The mix of familiar and overtly different made his excitement even greater. But he had a role to play here, and he needed to be calm and professional even though he'd love to charge out into the fields and run around like a demented toddler or ex-British Prime Minister.

Once the next wave had beamed down, they would travel a few kilometres on land to the rendezvous point. The Xoroans didn't have matter transportation technology, and at the moment the Chroalians weren't about to share. The agreement had been there would be a buffer zone because, unlike humans, the Xoroans had a lot more sophisticated scanning devices and limited space exploration under their belts.

The next wave from the *Endeavour* appeared and Zal almost

fell over his feet to get to him. His eyes were green and his tail twitching. "Are you all right? There was something wrong with the transporter."

Devlin could see it was taking all Zal's reserve not to reach out and touch him, to keep the distance between them respectful.

Dr Golic fixed Zal with a pointed look. "As you can see, Ambassador Taylor is perfectly all right. You can trust me to ensure he is well taken care of."

Devlin realised he was trying to be reassuring, Dr Golic being one of the few who knew of their relationship. "Honestly, Zal," Devlin said. "I'm fine."

Holjin grinned. "I even helped brush the dirt off, so he was in good hands."

Not a helpful interjection, but now wasn't the time and place to tell Holjin to back off. "Since we're all here and safe, I'd like to proceed. We don't want to be late for our hosts," Devlin said, hoping to put things back on track.

The overlander was a glorified armour-plated minibus that would seat them and their kit comfortably. Zal stuck to his side and claimed the seat next to him on the ground transport, which hadn't been in the original plan. Devlin was learning Zal had a fierce stubborn streak. He could see Zal was desperate to touch him and he squeezed his hand before letting go, hoping it would give some comfort.

He gave Devlin a small smile. "How's it feel to be on your first alien planet?"

"Good. I'm so happy that I've got the opportunity to see the universe, meet new species, alongside some special people."

The fields began to give way to the signs of urban sprawl, first with an occasional dwelling, but soon the collections of houses became denser. It wasn't a city in the sense of London or New York, in that there weren't towering skyscrapers, but there were roads, shops and office buildings, and as they got closer to the centre, the Xoroan escort vehicles, large trikes with armed officers, filtered in and flanked them either side and back and front. From Devlin's reading, the Xoroans had more infrastructure underground than on the surface, but he'd been provided scant information beyond there being an extensive cave system under all of the major cities. The farewell gala was planned for the Crimson Cavern and he couldn't wait to see what that was.

The transporter came to a halt outside a grand marble building that reminded Devlin a bit of St Paul's Cathedral due to its huge dome. Holjin was the first to stand. "As we said in the briefing session, we disembark in strict order." He looked at Zal. "You'll need to let Devlin go ahead of you and remain with the scientific party, initially, as the lead. You're not part of the ambassadorial group this time."

"Yes, Captain."

Zal hadn't requested a bigger involvement on the diplomatic front. He had a role to play and meetings scheduled with several academics and members of the government, and while he'd been happy with the assignment, now Devlin wasn't so sure Zal would want to be away from him so much.

He disembarked, falling into place behind the two senior crew members and next to Scrillia, who winked at him. They were in a courtyard. The gates to the palace had closed behind them as they entered, and while there were curious onlookers from the public staring through the railings, they were kept well away and were nowhere near the numbers he'd have expected if they'd been on Earth. An honour guard formed up the steps to the entrance and waiting for them was Filote, the First Minister of Xoros. She was tall by human standards, and as Devlin greeted her he realised they were near enough the same height.

"Welcome to Xoros, Ambassador Taylor. We are honoured to be the first planet you have visited."

His translator would pick up most of the hard work but he wanted to greet her in her own language. He bowed and said, "Tellek le shem."

Filote gasped and clapped in delight. "I am charmed that you have taken the pains to learn some words of our language."

"Not many, I'm afraid."

"But it shows your commitment." She took his arm, which he didn't think was protocol and made Scrillia raise an eyebrow. "I consider it my duty as your host to ensure you have a wonderful visit."

He'd expected a business-like greeting, not for him to be whisked inside on the arm of an alien, like an Austen-esque hero being led away to show off his footwork to the Ton. Because of his previous job, he'd been to plenty of welcome events and the schedule he was given suggested this would be no different, but instead of a room full of dignitaries, he, Holjin, and Scrillia were whisked away to what he assumed to be Filote's office.

"Madame Minister," began Scrillia, sounding bemused by the change of plan, "I don't believe we were to be separated from the rest of the party so soon."

Filote flapped her hand at Scrillia. "No need to twist your tail, Ambassador. Your people are being escorted to their rooms. You arrived a little later than we thought and so they are preparing for this evening. You will be able to join them once we have discussed a few items."

"Such as?" asked Holjin.

Folite wasn't paying much attention to the captain. She appeared more interested in Devlin. "If Ambassador Taylor is amenable, I wish to spend some time with him privately."

Devlin was all for building relations, but he had a line he wouldn't cross. "I'd be happy to. But it does depend on the topic—might be helpful to have a Chroalian with me."

"Earth's history with the accords is not too dissimilar to our own, I believe there are some learnings I could share." She leant in and sniffed him. "Tell me, are you mated? I'm unsure of human practices and would not wish to do anything that might be deemed inappropriate."

He bit his tongue to stop himself telling her she was too late for that, and it was Holjin who came to his defence. "Not publicly,

Madame Minister, but myself and Ambassador Taylor are in the early stages of an understanding."

Zal was going to kill him.

"Well, that is a pity, but I still wish to extend the offer to share our knowledge."

He could hardly refuse, but he would have to speak to Holjin; he didn't need someone coming to his rescue, especially in such a fashion. "I would gladly receive your wisdom."

She cackled and elbowed him in the ribs. "I'm sure you'll receive more than that from the captain. Do human males carry the children?"

"Thankfully not."

Scrillia hid her emotions well, though likely amused by the question, but Devlin also knew she would be aware that Zal would not be happy with this turn of events. Folite was oblivious to the chaos she had inadvertently caused with his love life, and he intended to keep it that way.

"I've assigned you all our best rooms. But would you prefer for Ambassador Taylor and Captain Holjin to share a suite?"

"No," Devlin answered quickly. "I mean it is a kind and considerate offer, but for my species, it is far too early in our relationship for us to spend the night together."

She raised an eyebrow. "You humans do have strange customs, but we must celebrate our differences."

"Ambassador Taylor is worth the wait," Holjin said with a grin.

"I do hope so, for your sake, Captain. Anyway, my staff will escort you to your rooms, and please join us for the reception."

From his grasp of how time worked on this planet, he had enough time for a quick shower and change of clothes before the reception started. He was looking forward to seeing Zal dressed up in his eveningwear, which reminded him he would need to catch him before the reception started.

The palace was a beautiful building, making him think of the stately homes of the peerage back in England. He was about to enter his suite when Holjin caught his arm. "If I could have a few moments before you get ready?"

"Of course, Captain."

The palace servant opened the door to his suite and retreated, leaving him alone with Holjin. The suite was as beautiful as the rest of the palace and several times the size of his room on board the *Endeavour*, and his bags had already been delivered and left on a low table.

"I think I owe you an apology, Devlin."

"I wish you hadn't alluded to us being in a relationship. I am more than capable of deflecting questions about my personal life."

Holjin looked contrite. "I know, and I am sorry, but at least this way you won't have to put up with the advances from the Xoroans. Believe it or not, they are even more direct than Chroalians."

"That wasn't in my briefing notes."

"It wouldn't have been considered something to be

concerned about for the rest of the team—I daresay several of the landing party will take the opportunity to further advance our cordial links. If you get my meaning."

"You make it sound like space exploration is one long sexual adventure."

Holjin grinned. "It can be. Most of the crew are single, like yourself. That's not to say we don't have a few couples who are committed only to each other, but if you want, there'll always be someone ready to play with you."

"If I'm ever interested, I can make my own arrangements, but now I've been put in a situation where I have to pretend we're somehow together."

Holjin shrugged. "The crew will know I only ever do temporary, so you'll still be considered a free agent. Although this evening, it'll be best for appearance's sake that I escort you to the reception."

He knew he didn't have much of a choice in the matter, but he'd hoped that tonight he and Zal could have made a first step towards being seen getting closer. They hadn't intended the Xoroan reception to be the official event they attended as a couple, rather that they would be seen being closer than just ambassador and his liaison, but now even that small baby step had been taken from them.

"I should tell Zal. We were going to arrive together since he is my liaison."

"Zal will understand. I'm sure there'll be a few techie types more than happy to keep our sexy xenobiologist company." Holjin winked. "He'll not be lonely."

"I didn't think of it in that way." He didn't like the sound of that one bit and tried to keep his emotion out of his voice. "He's not mentioned being interested in exploring those options when on Xoros."

"I can't see why he wouldn't. He's an energetic lover, and I'd hate to see him waste an opportunity." Holjin sauntered over to the door. "I'll be back to collect you. We can go down together."

He didn't need to know Holjin's opinions on Zal as a lover, but he had too many other things to sort out to dwell on it. Left alone, he wouldn't dawdle so he could get ready as quickly as possible and then see Zal. The shower in the bathroom was something special but he didn't have time to linger, and he hurtled back into his bedroom to find Zal sitting on his bed, dressed in his turquoise evening robes, looking beautiful but annoyed.

"Zal!"

"Mum told me that the Xoroans think you're Holjin's new plaything." Zal could do pissy very well.

"Not exactly, and I'm not any happier about it than you. Especially as according to Holjin, all single Chroalians have the reputation of wanting to fuck their way across the universe and you'd be no different."

"You know that's not true about me! At least, not anymore."

Devlin grabbed his tuxedo from one of his bags, amazed at the Chroalian technology's ability to keep things crease-free. "And you know I have no interest in Holjin."

Zal huffed and threw himself back on the bed. "I'm sorry. I'm a being a herrectsac's arsehole. I'd planned we'd spend this evening getting close and now I have to watch Holjin in the place I want to be."

"I kinda hoped you'd still be close by. It is my first alien off-world soiree and even if we can't be a couple openly yet, we know we are."

Zal rolled onto his side. "Yeah, all that fuzziness is mine. Is that a new dinner jacket?"

The cut was a little closer than his old one. "Yes, what do you think?"

Zal's eyes were turning purple. "I think I'm going to need to sneak in here after the party and fuck your brains out."

He was an unmitigated tease. "You can't say things like that. How am I meant to get through an evening pretending to be interested in Holjin knowing that I could be with you instead?"

"At least you know I will be thinking of doing unspeakable things to you rather than having any interest in a Xoroan." Zal rolled off the bed and gave him a quick kiss. "I best get back. The science team are all meeting together to go downstairs, and now I haven't got my favourite fuzzy human escort, I'd best go join them."

Devlin would have much preferred to spend the evening with Zal by his side but equally he was excited about his first ambassadorial duty on an alien planet. "Holjin will be back soon to collect me. But don't forget your promise. If you don't sneak in here later, I will be very upset."

Zal had only been gone a few minutes when Holjin arrived. Holjin looked amazing in his dress uniform, a well-cut robe similar to Zal's; however, Holjin managed to look like he'd been born to wear it. If Devlin had been a single man, he would have had no trouble in accepting Holjin's advances, and it was only his devotion to Zal that allowed him to maintain his distance.

"My word, Devlin, don't you look dashing," Holjin said. "You'll thank me for pretending we're together, because there is no way you wouldn't have received ridiculous amounts of attention and requests to fuck you."

Devlin spluttered at Holjin's brazenness. "I beg your pardon?"

"Come now, Devlin, surely you don't think they'll want to hold your hand? I mean I would love to hold your hand, but I would love to do a lot more as I was holding it."

"I have told you I am not interested."

Holjin chuckled. "I know, and I will behave myself. You have my word."

They headed back downstairs and were directed towards the back of the palace where the staterooms were located. Devlin could tell a great deal of time and effort had been put into the preparation and knew there was a small army of beleaguered staff behind the scenes, all working hard to make sure absolutely nothing would be allowed to go wrong.

There must have already been about a hundred people waiting for them to arrive; all of the Chroalian delegation was already assembled, as were many senior Xoroan politicians. In fact, looking around, it dawned on Devlin that he and the captain were the last to arrive, and it would be obvious they had done so as a couple, meaning the rumours would be racing through the ship within the hour. He could already hear in his head the endless chatter of the ensigns all vying to get Captain Holjin's sloppy seconds. Folite spotted them and headed over in their direction.

"You two make for quite the wonderful couple. Perfect match, I'd say." She grabbed two multi-coloured drinks off a waiter's tray as he glided past. "You must try this. It is something of a delicacy from this city."

He hid his displeasure at the so-called compliment by taking a sip of the drink. From the colour, he'd expected it to be fruity but it was more spicy, reminding him of sandalwood and ginger. It wasn't unpleasant but he couldn't say he'd want a second. He also didn't want Holjin's hand on the base of his spine, and he took a deliberate step away to remove it. It was going to be a long night.

Folite's eyes narrowed for a moment. "Holjin, I wondered if you would be interested in a display of dancing."

She didn't give Holjin time to answer and two beautiful women took him by an arm each and escorted him away, not that he argued. Folite turned to Devlin. "I do hope I did not misconstrue something, but the captain appeared to be making you uncomfortable."

Devlin supposed it was her ability to read people that made her a great politician. "My species is more reserved. In the early stages of an understanding, we are not used to public displays of affection, whereas the Chroalians are far bolder."

"My people are more like the Chroalians in that respect, but once we are aware someone is not available, most of us would not press further. And let us remember ambassadorial duties do not make you a prostitute—you do not have to let anyone touch you that you do not want. "

"Sounds like a voice of experience."

"I would say it is ingrained in us as a species." She took hold of his elbow and gently guided him to one side. "Earth is not so different to Xoros; our people and humans embarked on a similar path to the stars. We too were limited by the accords, and it took us a long time before we were allowed our freedom."

"I don't believe my people are ready—a handful of us might be, but most are too angry with one another. Until we can make peace between ourselves, we aren't fit to make nice with others."

"We've had many wars on Xoros, but most were caused by inequality, and some of those policing the accords couldn't see that by helping us we could eradicate the injustices quicker."

"I see."

He kept his tone neutral. She appeared to be giving him a subtle warning, and he knew better than to think it would be more flagrant in public, but she had alluded to wanting to discuss things with Devlin earlier, and he would probe more when they got the chance.

"I think you do, Devlin. Now, we should... how do you say it? Mingle."

Chapter Twelve

As Zal observed Captain Holjin in his rightful spot next to Devlin he couldn't say he liked him much. He'd watched with growing annoyance as Holjin seemed to think he had the right to put his hand on Devlin, and every time Devlin would move away, they'd share pointed looks and Holjin would back off, but only for a while.

To quell his burgeoning anger, he grabbed another drink and turned back to the pretty Xoroan who was a soil physicist. She had dusky pink skin with feather shading down the side of her face. He'd started the evening in a larger group, but the others had peeled away as couples as the night went on, leaving just him and Nexi.

"I was reading that Chroalians have unique scale patterns. Is that true?"

He'd been distracted by his thoughts about Devlin and only now realised Nexi was trying to flirt with him. His species were renowned for their friendliness until they were paired, and she would have no reason to think Zal wasn't available or interested, especially as he'd ended up with just the two of them talking.

"Yes, a bit like a fingerprint. Not only the pattern but colours as well." He tried to sound matter-of-fact, but the way she bit her lip suggested that wasn't the message he was sending. "Not that exciting."

"I also heard that your eyes change colour depending on the emotion you're encountering." She leant in closer and whispered into his ear. "I'd love to see them when you come."

At that exact moment, Devlin looked in his direction, and he saw a look of confusion, perhaps even hurt. Nexi was pressed against him, her hand on his stomach and he'd done nothing to discourage her, mainly because he'd been caught off guard. But that wasn't much of an excuse.

He stepped away. "Sorry, I... I should see how Ambassador Taylor is doing. I'm his assigned liaison officer, and this is his first evening on a new world."

"Surely Captain Holjin can take care of him. You can help build relations between our people in another way."

He doubted she knew the meaning of the word subtle, and he needed to get to Devlin. "I don't want to be accused of shirking my duties."

She pouted as he hurried towards Devlin, who had now been

cornered by the Minister of Soil Propagation. "So you see, Ambassador, there's a great deal of science to ensuring the nutrients are balanced."

"Minister Rael, I see you are helping to educate Ambassador Taylor on the key to the planet's success."

"Lieutenant Catenmir, I am looking forward to spending some time with your team tomorrow. I know Nexi is excited—I saw you were already becoming acquainted."

Zal glanced at Devlin, who seemed to be waiting for his answer. "I had intended to accompany Ambassador Taylor tomorrow. I have been assigned as his liaison, and I need to ensure that his inaugural visit goes to plan."

"An admirable sentiment."

"Also, Nexi's speciality is more in line with Teric's, so I had thought to pair them up." He hadn't thought about it until a few moments ago but it seemed the perfect solution. "Their academic collaboration may help with the fingfick beetle issue."

Rael made a series of clicking noises, denoting he was excited. "I should go and tell Nexi; anything that will help eradicate the pest will be warmly received."

He scurried away and Zal smiled at Devlin. "How's the evening going?"

"Better now Holjin is being entertained by dancing girls and my special friend is no longer being draped over by a beautiful alien."

"I did not invite her attention." He reached out to touch

Devlin, then realised the act would look far too intimate. "My species has a reputation for being friendly."

"I know, and if I thought you'd encouraged her, we would be having a very different conversation."

He stepped as close as he dared. "Chroalians have a different view on intimacy to your species, but once we attach ourselves to a mate or mates, we tend to be exclusive within that relationship. And I would consider myself attached."

Devlin's eyes sparkled. "I am glad to hear it. Do you think we have done our duty for the evening?"

Zal glanced around: the crowds were thinning, and there was still enough daylight to see a little of the palace's grounds. "I think so. Would you like to have a stroll outside before you retire for the evening?"

He'd not got to spend much time with Devlin today, and he'd missed him. "I read the Xoroans rarely grow plants that don't have a non-economic use, and the palace is one of the rare places that does, so I would love to see something I might not otherwise get the chance to."

Zal had thought to sneak into Devlin's room, but he'd considered the idea too great a risk with so many people in the palace and the heightened security, so this would be his only chance of the evening to have a kiss and a cuddle. "I reckon there'll be some wonderful examples of plants that grow in secluded areas."

"Then I definitely want to see them."

Zal was relieved that no one tried to intervene as they left. "I don't know if it's a good idea if I come to your room. I want to, but we could get caught."

"I know. Let's see, but for now, we'll just have to make the most of our time." Devlin reached up and stroked his ear, and Zal had to stop himself from purring.

"What did you think of your first alien planet?" he asked, trying to get his mind off the thought of fucking Devlin in a bush.

"So far so good. It's surreal to think I am here when less than a month ago I was back on Earth—alone and miserable."

He could echo the sentiments. "I was going slowly mad without you. Nothing I did worked, my experiments failed, none of my calculations added up. I was a shadow of myself. There seemed to be little point in seeing the universe if the most important being in it was the one I couldn't have."

"Now we can see the universe together—you can help me not put my foot in it, and I can help you reclaim your work-life balance."

Zal thought his translator must be malfunctioning. "What are you putting your foot in?"

"Sorry, another colloquialism...from putting your foot in your mouth. It means to say the wrong thing." Zal wrinkled his nose and Devlin laughed. "I didn't say it made sense."

The gardens were glorious by moonlight, the shadows adding an extra dimension to their beauty. Zal kept his distance until they rounded a secluded corner and then crowded up close to Devlin. "You do not know how much I wanted to grab you and kiss you this evening."

"I gathered from some of your pointed stares at the captain. You might need to tone it down a little—Sihil has noticed something is going on."

If anyone was going to, it would be her. "I'll try my best, but tonight was meant to be ours, and the captain stole our chance."

"She noticed before this evening. Apparently, you were joking with a couple of ensigns yesterday about me and their plans to entice me into a three-way and how I was too fine a specimen to be an easy conquest."

Devlin didn't sound happy and Zal wasn't sure why. "Well you are, but it was just banter. Common on a ship like the *Endeavour*."

Devlin shook his head. "I think she took your comments to mean you were also interested in me, and you can't go around acting like that."

"Devlin, given what Chroalians are like, it would be strange that I wasn't." He grinned. "And I am very interested in getting close to you. Pity I can't be closer at the moment. I should get a kiss to make things bearable."

"You are the most ridiculous creature."

"That was not a no."

Devlin leant in and kissed him and Zal's tail quivered in delight. He'd like nothing more than to disappear into the bushes with Devlin, get prickled in all the right places and come out looking smug, but if they were caught, they'd be in so much shit a quick fumble wasn't worth it.

They parted and Zal's head spun, a little lightheaded from the effects of Devlin's kisses. While they still had so much to learn about each other, there was no denying their physical compatibility. "We should get to bed. We've a busy couple of days ahead of us and if I don't stop now, I'm going to cause a diplomatic incident," Zal said.

He took hold of Devlin's hand and pulled him to his feet, not letting go until they were closer to the palace.

"Sleep well, Ambassador Taylor," he said outside Devlin's door.

"You too, Lieutenant Catenmir."

Back in his room Zal pouted; he'd wanted to spend longer with Devlin, for them to have spent his first night on an alien planet at least partly together. He stomped into the bathroom all set to have a wank in the shower, but he didn't want that. He wanted Devlin, and fuck it, he was going to have him.

Chapter Thirteen

D evlin carefully undressed. He'd need the dinner jacket for the farewell event and had been given a fancy cleaning sleeve to put it in by one of the ship's stewards, with instructions that the sleeve would make it fresh and clean for when he needed it next. He'd been amazed at the host of little bits of technology that made the Chroalians' day-to-day lives easier. No dashing to dry cleaners or worrying about running out of items, because they had everything covered.

He wondered how different daily life was outside the regiment of serving aboard a spaceship like *Endeavor*. Would it be more like Earth, where everything, at least in his life, held a thin veneer of order overlaying a bag of chaotic cats? Zal didn't strike him as the type who would be structured and ordered outside of his job. He had a freeness about him that would never be fully caged—or maybe that was just his tail.

The Xoroan mission had been an amazing first experience on a new planet, and while he would have preferred to have ended it in a different way, he had to accept that he couldn't have everything. He stripped off the rest of his clothes and was planning to shower when there was a soft knock on his door. Grabbing a dressing gown, he tentatively opened the door. Zal stood there grinning, dressed in casual clothes.

"Complementary massage service, sir?"

He ushered Zal inside. "I hope no one saw you?"

"No, I was sneaky, and I would have come up with an excuse if I was stopped." Zal wrapped his arms around Devlin's neck and kissed him. "Now, that is better."

"You said something about a massage?"

Zal grinned and waved his tail. "You'll find that with our extra appendage, we Chroalians give some of the best massages. Guaranteed results. And I do like to ensure I give my favourite client the very, very best."

Devlin was all up for a bit of masseuse and client role-play. "What results are you guaranteeing?"

"I would say the ultimate relaxation, but I intend to rile you up good and proper."

Zal groaned as he ran his hand down Devlin's chest and Devlin adored the effect his fuzziness had on him. He was walked backwards and, with a firm push, landed flat on his back, his dressing gown open, and all of him on display. The way Zal looked at him made him feel sexy and desired. No other lover had ever made him feel so wanted.

Zal stripped off and sat astride him. "Is this all part of the service? You being naked?"

"Oh yes, how am I going to make sure every part of you is taken care of if I'm dressed?"

Zal rolled his hips, rubbing their cocks together, and then ran the tip of his tail up and down Devlin's inner thigh. "Fuck! That's an intimate massage."

"I also like to focus on specific areas. Anyone can do a decent job of a back massage but they can't do what I can."

Devlin loved Zal's boldness, but he also loved that he had a gland that meant he was self-lubricating. Devlin's cock throbbed and Zal teased his hole with the tip of his tail. They'd not done that before and the sensation was amazing. He would probably need proper preparation to go further, but the future idea of letting Zal fuck him with his tail made him desperate for more.

Devlin almost lost his mind as Zal took hold of the base of Devlin's cock and sank down. He was a fucking beautiful creature. Zal's scales rippled under his hands and he held onto Zal's hips as he rode him. Devlin had never felt so alive, the mix of Zal's slightly cooler body temperature encasing his cock and his clever tail teasing his rim pushed Devlin closer and closer to the edge. He bit down on his lip to try to stop himself from being so loud, and Zal was gasping as he used Devlin exactly how he wanted to get his own pleasure.

Devlin wrapped his hand around Zal's cock and pumped him firmly, the soft bristle of his scales an additional sensation he couldn't hold back any longer and he came, hard. The world exploded behind his eyes as Zal cried out, ribbons of his light-blue release covering Devlin's belly.

It took several minutes for the world to right itself as they exchanged filthy kisses, clinging together. "You are amazing," Devlin said, panting as he tried to steady his breathing. "And your tail... fucking hell."

Zal's eyes glowed yellow. "You liked it?"

"Yeah, I *really* liked it. I'd like to explore playing a bit more."

"Oh, Devlin, I'd like that too." Zal's tail slithered across his belly. "It's a matter of good prep, but I'd love to experiment."

They lay there for a while, Devlin enjoying having Zal in his arms, and he wished he'd been able to hold him in public. They shared another languid kiss. "I'm sorry Holjin opened his big mouth," Devlin said. "I would have much preferred you to have been the one protecting my honour."

"It's not your fault, and we'll make up for it on the next planet. It's Dyun. I've been before and it has the most amazing twin sun system. The sunsets are to die for."

"The sort of thing that would drive me into the arms of a certain sexy xenobiologist?"

"You would be forgiven for not being able to control yourself." Zal kissed him again. "I'd better go. I'm sure there'll be several people creeping about between rooms so I'll need to be careful."

Zal dressed and, with a final kiss, snuck out of Devlin's room. He couldn't wait until they wouldn't have to sneak around, when he could wake up with Zal's tail wrapped around his middle, and be known as Zal's partner. They had plenty to do on Xoros, but Devlin couldn't help but wish they were closer to Dyun, to see the amazing sunset, and complete his plans to publicly take Zal into his arms and kiss him breathless.

Chapter Fourteen

Devlin had spent much of the morning on a tour of an agricultural museum, not the most thrilling of excursions and made worse by the absence of Zal, who was supposed to be with him, but one of the Xoroans had been insistent his scientific knowledge was needed and so that was the end of that. Holjin had either been genuinely excited about crop rotation or he was a marvellous actor, and somehow Scrillia had been able to avoid it altogether.

He'd stopped to examine a large metal object that was somewhere between a boat propeller and a large knife. Filote glided up to him and took his elbow. "It is a harvesting head for long-stemmed arable crops. Perhaps, Ambassador, you'd like me to talk you through the accords exhibition."

"In an agricultural museum?"

"Yes, our world and its history cannot be separated from our farming heritage." She did not speak again until they were on their own in a small exhibition room which was lined with glass-fronted cabinets. She tapped one pane of glass, indicating a scroll that had been mounted for display. "This scroll contains the original permission that allowed us to begin our interstellar explorations. We were denied support from those who wrote the accords for many years, them citing our backward agricultural ways as a reason why we should remain limited to our own planet."

She'd mentioned the accords to him yesterday, and he was bright enough to know there was more behind it. "You believe your people were unduly held back?"

"Yes, the Union of Planets' accords council discusses whether a race is worthy. They are overly conservative and somewhat protectionary."

"You would expect them to want to protect their people."

She made a soft snort. "Some of them don't want to protect their people from a hostile species but more from one that might be competition or propose different ideologies. The Chroalians, in general, I trust, but every race has reasons for how they conduct themselves, and none in my experience are altruistic."

"I could say the same for Earth. We're not wanting to explore space for the benefit of anyone other than ourselves. We've seen what the universe can offer from the aliens we granted settlers status to."

She smiled at him. "And the same for Xoros, although we are not a planet that houses refugees, we are one that helps to feed them and aids starving worlds. But don't you see, we were, and you are, being held accountable to a higher bar than those who drew up the accords?"

"However, it is their party and they know they can invite who they want, stipulate the dress code, and request a dish for the buffet."

She laughed and took his arm. "A perfect analogy. It's understandable when some of the earlier guests were not well behaved, but then, instead of them being ejected, they were invited to help draw up the house rules."

Devlin knew that diplomacy was not known for straight talk, and he suspected Filote thought he knew more than he did. "I'm not sure what you are trying to warn me about. I don't know of anyone directly hostile to Earth beginning to explore."

"They aren't going to be obvious, are they? Devlin, I have heard rumours that it would be in the best interests of many people for your ambassadorial role to be unsuccessful."

He needed to be careful, as false friends could be as dangerous as obvious enemies. "I'm not sure I follow."

"Earth is relatively primitive. As was Xoros. You being allowed to wander about as an ambassador for your primitive society might give other planets the idea that they could too. A high profile failure and the accords working to prevent wider fallout would serve the narrative very well."

"But why would Xoros care if I, and by extension, Earth fails?"

She led him over to another part of the exhibition. A memorial marking an incident where ten thousand Xoroans lost their lives in fires on the subcontinent. "We were denied protection; the council said interference was not allowed. If we had been members, they would have stepped in, but they didn't."

There was more here than a natural disaster taking its toll. "Protection? Those were deliberate fires?"

"Hostile forces. So you see, Xoros does not want to see it repeated. Earth has more protection already than we did because of the service you do housing refugees, but do not think the UoP will care too much if you are attacked."

"I need to make sure that I do not fail."

"I do not have a full picture, but there are whispers of tests and trials to see if you are cut out to be Earth's Ambassador and if your people are worthy to reach the stars."

"I am being tested? By the Chroalians?"

"I don't know. Maybe, or maybe they are also being tested. Scrillia is someone I trust—you are safe with her. Just keep your eyes open and your wits sharp."

Voices from the other members of their party made Filote glance in their direction. Holjin appeared with the Xoroan Minister for Internal Affairs.

"Ah, here you are," Holjin said, sauntering over and rubbing Devlin's cheek with the tip of his tail. "Ready to leave? We've a luncheon with members of the Infection Control Bureau."

Filote checked her watch. "Where has the time gone?"

No one would have guessed from her expression what they'd been speaking about, and Devlin needed time to think. He'd discuss what she'd said with Zal as soon as he could as he had no reason to doubt Filote's motivation, and he needed to confirm if someone was trying to sabotage him and then, if so, make sure he gave them no reason to send him home to Earth in disgrace.

*

Zal had been impressed by the quality of the research he'd seen. The Xoroans weren't considered highly advanced but the work they were doing on crop production would be valuable to many planets and could be used to eradicate hunger in several situations. They had a considered approach to pest control as well, careful not to pollute their water or to screw up other aspects of their ecosystems. Chroalia hadn't been that forward-looking and it had taken decades, even when the technology was available, to reverse the issues their earlier scientists had caused.

He would be meeting the rest of the Chroalian delegation for dinner, and as excited as Devlin had been about his first planet, Zal didn't think he'd been that interested in the life cycle of the fingfick beetle or calcium recycling, so he would be best kept away from some of his fellow techies.

Zal took a shower, loving the water pressure, and used the amazing body lotion that had been left in his room. When he emerged from the bathroom, Devlin was sitting on the edge of his bed, not looking like the excitable man he'd left at breakfast.

"Devlin, is there something wrong?"

"I need to talk to you. Or someone. I've been given information that is rather worrying."

"Let me put some clothes on, I sense this is a conversation that nakedness won't help."

Devlin chuckled. "A rare beast."

A few minutes later, dressed, he sat next to Devlin on the bed and took hold of his hand. "So what's got you all worried?"

"Filote engineered time with me on my own at the museum so she could speak to me."

Devlin was an attractive man, he wouldn't be surprised if Filote was interested, but Zal would have thought Holjin would be a deterrent. "I thought she'd backed off."

"She wasn't after my body, Zal. She wanted to warn me of a potential problem. She said she'd heard someone was trying to sabotage me and my mission to prevent, or at least delay, Earth's interstellar hopes."

There were many things he might have guessed Devlin would say, but that wasn't one of them. "That doesn't make any sense. Why and who would want to do that?"

"She didn't say who, beyond inferring heavily it was linked to someone who policed the accords. As for the why, she said it was to prevent too many others from getting the same idea."

Zal shook his head. "There's a need to protect in both directions. Those not ready to leave their planet, and those already out there, from hostile civilisations who might be far enough advanced but would cause trouble."

"That wasn't the inference. And she was clear that she trusted the Chroalians, so she's not accusing your people, but she wanted to warn me."

"Then why?"

"She didn't say why exactly, but I think she meant that the more people that explore, the less importance the individual members might have, and that's a political motivation. When I think about it, we have parallels in Earth's history. The colonial powers, and my country was one of the worst offenders—built empires and wanted to control them. Her warning makes sense in that context."

Zal puffed out his cheeks as he thought. He could understand Devlin's reasoning, but he was applying the way humans acted to an alien race. "I can't say we have anything parallel on Chroalia in the last thousand years. Prior to that, then yes, but you wouldn't apply the standards of something a millennia ago to what's happening now."

"So you don't think I should give much credence to what Filote said?"

His first thought was to deny it but a tingle at the base of his tail made him pause. "As a scientist, you should fully investigate a hypothesis before it is dismissed."

"Look, I'm not naïve enough to follow Filote blindly, but there's something I can't shake here, and I might be overthinking things."

"Such as?" Zal asked. Devlin wasn't the sort of man to take things at face value; he was intuitive and capable of feats of deduction that many others weren't.

"Our imaginary guests, the hiccough with the transporter, and the unexpected delays setting up a secure channel for my correspondence with Earth."

The transporter and the communications channel he could have explained as normal blips aboard ship but together, and then in context with the fake boarding party, Devlin might be onto something.

"We should talk to my mum. But when we're back on board the ship and in her consulting rooms because those have high-security encryption so it would be difficult for someone to listen in."

Devlin looked relieved. "Thank you for not dismissing me."

"Never. We're in this together, Devlin. If there is something going on we have to make sure we stop it, because as much as I'd like to see Earth succeed in its objectives, I'm selfish and don't want to lose you."

Devlin kissed him and it took all Zal's effort not to push him backwards and for them to forget they were supposed to be going downstairs for dinner. Devlin was a wonderful man, and Zal adored him. There was no way he was going to let anyone come between them and that included the accord council members.

Chapter Fifteen

Devlin stared out across the Crimson Cavern—he'd never seen anything like it in his life. The walls of the circular expanse were covered in red crystals that were similar to rubies found on Earth, and the lighting bathed everything in a red glow. There must have been at least three hundred people gathered, and waiters circulated with platters of local delicacies, for which Devlin had been sent a menu beforehand so he would be aware of what he'd be eating.

"Isn't it spectacular?" Holjin asked. The captain had been at his side for all of their events and had thankfully ceased to be as tactile with his hands, but his tail, on the other hand, wrapped around Devlin's waist at every opportunity. "It's quite something to experience on your first planet."

"Are you telling me, this is as amazing for you as for me?

You've not seen anything similar in all your adventures?"

"Every place has something unique. The main enjoyment of exploring is seeing new things, comparing them to others isn't necessary."

"I suppose that's one way never to get bored of your job."

Holjin laughed. "I'm not sure I'm capable of being bored. Even on planets I've been to before, I can't have seen everything. An open mind means there's no room for boredom."

Devlin was impressed by Holjin's attitude, and as a captain, in general. If he could learn to keep his tail to himself, Devlin could imagine them becoming friends.

"I hope to mimic and maintain such a spirit."

"I'd expect nothing less from Earth's first ambassador."

They were joined by one of Filote's ministers. Yahi, who looked after transport, was a beautiful woman with a dusty pink spiral over her cheek. "Ambassador Taylor, I hope you have enjoyed your time with us. How did you find your visit to a planet not your own?"

He had so many expectations and fears. Worries about whether he would come across as a bumbling idiot or would inadvertently cause some sort of incident had not come to pass, and instead, he'd had a marvellous time. Never in his wildest dreams did he think he'd be exploring the stars, and here he was, standing between two different aliens light years from Earth. "I've been blessed that Xoros was my first experience. Your planet is beautiful and your hospitality warm and welcoming."

"You have been a wonderful guest. Filote was singing your praises this morning, and I do think it a brilliant idea that you are taking your inaugural steps with the Chroalians. Ambassador Scrillia is well respected."

Earth wasn't in a position to do anything other than piggyback another species. "I hope to learn a great deal from her."

The conversation seemed to repeat itself many times throughout the evening as Devlin spoke to different politicians. Unlike on Earth, there didn't seem to be much in the way of celebrities, or at least they weren't deemed important enough to meet with him, whether this was because the Xoroans were more enlightened than humans or not he wouldn't like to say.

He had been warned the cavern could get a little claustrophobic, and Dr Golic had said that the air quality might not be optimal for his lung capacity so he should take at least one break to the surface. A servant escorted him to a shortcut to a service elevator, and he was surprised when Zal caught up with him. "Is everything all right?"

"I'm going to get a breath of air."

"I'll come with you." Zal's tail flicked, and Devlin knew that sign. If all went well he could get in a quick snog before they had to return. "I don't want you getting lost on your last evening."

They entered the lift and ascended, and less than a minute later, another servant opened the doors and guided them out onto a secluded platform where, Devlin realised, if they went to the end they'd be hidden by an outcrop of rock. By Zal's grin, he'd had the same idea, and he took his hand, then dragged him over. The night sky was a deep velvety purple, the stars twinkling. Devlin was surprised by the lack of light pollution.

Zal wormed his tail under Devlin's jacket, and Devlin let Zal take him into his arms. "We don't have long, but I had to get a few moments with you," Zal said, rubbing his nose against Devlin's. "You've been so good the last few days. I know we've some things to look into when we're back on the ship, but you've made a wonderful first impression. I'm so proud of you."

Zal's lips were soft as they kissed, and Devlin couldn't wait until they were at a point when they wouldn't have to steal time together.

"Gentlemen, what is going on here?"

Devlin and Zal sprang apart at the sound of Holjin's voice. "I was ensuring that Ambassador Taylor was safe, Captain. He was in need of some air."

"I don't think he needed you to deliver oxygen directly to his lungs, Lieutenant Catenmir."

"No, Captain."

"You are consenting adults, but I must remind you that the Xoroans are under the impression that Ambassador Taylor is in a relationship with me. If you were to be caught in the position you were just in by someone else, it would not reflect well on those involved. Understood?"

Devlin knew where Holjin was going with this, and he had a point. There would be comments made about whether he was trustworthy or, if he could sneak behind the back of the captain who had welcomed him on board his ship, who else would he be capable of betraying? "We didn't mean to be so indelicate."

Holjin stared between them. "Oh, this is not the first time."

Zal stood in front of Devlin, and he would let Zal lead here as the Chroalian. This was his culture, and he was, in theory, the liaison to the ambassador. If he wanted to deny what was happening between them, then Devlin would follow, but he didn't think Holjin would believe them. "No, Captain. But I don't think this is the place to discuss the situation."

Holjin didn't look upset, but Devlin couldn't read him. Although, he was glad Zal had decided not to hide.

"I agree. We return to the *Endeavour* in the morning. As the serving officer, I will expect Lieutenant Catenmir to report to me when instructed to explain what is going on."

"Yes, Captain," Zal replied, his tone clipped.

"Back to the cavern. Now." Holjin shook his head. "Keep your distance. Actually, Devlin, you stay with me."

Zal tilted his head up and stared Holjin in the eye. "I would appreciate it, Captain, that you keep your tail to yourself."

Devlin knew that had been bothering Zal.

"There are a number of things that are beginning to make sense. Rest assured, Zal, I will not lay a scale on Devlin."

Holjin dropping the formality was a deliberate message, and Devlin didn't think the captain would have an issue with their relationship, but more that he would have liked to have been informed first.

They followed Holjin back to the cavern in silence, and once at the celebration, Zal went to join his fellow scientists. Holjin took hold of Devlin's arm—there was nothing romantic in the gesture. "Come on, Devlin. There are many here who will want to wish you safe travels."

Chapter Sixteen

D evlin paced his cabin. Holjin discovering them in mid-embrace was a minor distraction compared to the bigger problem he was ruminating over. The door to his cabin opened and Zal arrived. "I spoke to my mum and she's available now. We need to head to her consulting rooms."

They'd agreed not to talk across the computer system. Devlin's view was they should try to reduce any chance of tracking. Even though it was obvious Zal had thought him a little odd, Devlin couldn't shake some of the training he'd received in his early years with the Ministry of Alien Relations, where he'd learnt to be circumspect when not knowing who was friend or foe. He didn't necessarily think it was the Chroalians, or at least not the ones on board, as they appeared to believe they had been boarded and, in his experience, faking those kinds of reactions took a great deal of acting skill.

They entered Scrillia's rooms. Devlin had already spent several hours in here since joining the crew, and there was something about them that settled him. Whether it was the little ornaments that were so uniquely Scrillia or the way their previous conversations had been conducted, or even the arrangement of the furniture, he couldn't say, but he felt safe here and confident he would be listened to without reproach.

"There you are," she said. She didn't stand and motioned for them to sit in the swivel chairs in front of her. "Zal tells me you have something on your mind, Devlin."

"I hope I don't come across as too reactionary. I believe myself to be a calm and considered individual, but I was told something while on Xoros that has troubled me."

"I've not known you long, Devlin. But I can tell when someone has the ability to judge their situation correctly without panic, so I doubt you'd ever be called reactionary."

He was relieved to hear her say that, and her opinion of him mattered a great deal to him for several reasons, not just because she was his boyfriend's mother. "Filote took great pains to speak to me alone, wanting to warn me of a potential threat to my role and therefore Earth's ambitions."

Scrillia sat further back in her chair. "She is another level-headed individual. Not one for grandiose actions or hysterics, but at the same time she will have her own reasons to act. In what way does this threat manifest?"

Devlin felt rather like he was speaking to a psychiatrist, which had been part of his annual health check when he had been assigned to active service. "She didn't give specifics, but instead, she said she had heard rumours there were some people who would think it better if I failed."

"Do you have reasons apart from what she said to make you think there could be any truth in her beliefs? I can't imagine you would be bringing this to me in isolation."

Zal sat forwards. "We've discussed this together and, if you consider the boarding party that wasn't there, the issues setting up Devlin's communication back to Earth, and the blip with the transporter, it all begins to add up."

"Three things that individually wouldn't normally be linked together," Scrillia said carefully. "I can see, though, that they possibly could be. But that doesn't prove anything, nor does it suggest a motive."

"Filote said it was to discourage other races who might only be on the cusp of space exploration from doing so."

She was quiet for a moment. "It can be a crowded universe. I imagine some might not like the field to be more so."

Devlin was surprised by her change of stance. "You believe what Filote said?"

"It is more that I know not every member of the UoP council wanted the Earth Ambassador programme to start so soon."

"But enough to stop me now I've started?"

"Of that, I'm not sure, but there were members who doubted

humans would ever be ready to leave their planet. No one said that to me directly, but then, I have been a vocal supporter of Earth."

"So you would not be someone who would be actively sought out to discuss the matter."

Scrillia smiled. "Correct. But that does not stop me from making some enquiries of those who might have been approached and who would subsequently talk to me."

"Is there anything we should do in the meantime?" Devlin pressed. "I can't imagine that is something you could do quickly."

"You can be quick, or you can be subtle, and I think the latter is what we want here," she said with a wry smile. "Although the next planet is not a diplomatic visit, we are attending a conference, and I should be able to have a few side conversations."

"So we should wait?" Devlin asked. They would be in orbit of Dyun within seven Chroalian days.

"I'm not sure what else you can do at this point. You could speak to Holjin—he might have his own suspicions, as I know he wasn't happy about the fake boarding party, and I would see him as an ally."

Zal wrinkled his nose. "I don't think I'm the captain's favourite at the moment."

Scrillia tutted. "Zal, you need to put this jealousy of yours to one side."

"It's not that," Zal said. They hadn't told Scrillia that they'd been caught.

The computer beeped. "Message for Lieutenant Catenmir

from Captain Holjin."

"Talk of the devil," muttered Devlin, and both Scrillia and Zal looked at him in confusion. "Earth saying—don't worry about it."

Zal sighed and answered. "Put him through."

"My ready room, Lieutenant. Now." Holjin didn't wait for a reply.

Scrillia raised an eyebrow. "What have you done?"

"Devlin can fill you in. I'd better go and face down the captain and his ego now he knows he won't get to wrap his tail around my boyfriend."

Zal hurried and Scillia turned to Devlin. "Well?"

*

Zal was surprised Holjin had waited so long once they were back on the ship to demand his presence. He supposed it was only the risk that an outsider might have heard their conversation that had discouraged him from ripping into him while still on the planet. He stood in the formal pose expected in the situation, hands behind his back and his feet hip-width apart.

"I want an explanation, Lieutenant Catenmir, for your behaviour down on Xoros."

"I'm not sure what you are referring to, Captain," Zal replied, determined to only answer exactly what he was asked.

"Playing dumb doesn't suit you. I want to know the nature of your relationship with Ambassador Taylor." Holjin took a step closer so he was standing directly in front of Zal. "I want the truth."

He could try to bluff his way out of this, tell Holjin they were just starting out as a couple, but somehow it didn't feel right to lie about what it was he and Devlin had. Also, the captain wasn't easily fooled, and Zal couldn't afford to get permanently on his bad side. "Devlin's my partner, and the only thing we've done wrong is not be circumspect on one occasion. If all goes well, I hope to make him my bond-mate."

"Bond-mate?" spluttered Holjin. "He hasn't been on the ship more than a few days."

"We met first when I was down on Earth. He got under my scales, and I thought I'd never see him again. Then the Ambassador Programme happened, and I got to have Devlin back."

Holjin opened and closed his mouth a few times. "But that was still hardly any time. Wait... are you telling me he's in the role because of you?"

Zal's tail lashed violently at the insinuation. "Firstly, I don't expect someone who has never experienced or even wished to experience love, to understand. Secondly, Devlin was already on the shortlist, and he would not have been given the position if he were not the best human for the job."

"I suppose you're not the type to fall head over tail for someone substandard. But I need to ensure the safety of this ship and its diplomatic mission."

"Devlin will only be a benefit to the *Endeavour*. You've seen his capabilities. The reason you're annoyed is because you want to fuck him—although that's hardly a ringing endorsement from you, given you're not exactly picky."

Holjin scowled. "Lieutenant, this is neither the time nor place for those sorts of comments."

"Apologies, Captain, but you may have noticed that I have been a little protective of him, not wanting to be left out of plans that involved him. Your obvious intentions towards Devlin have brought out instincts I wasn't aware I had."

"I would never have thought you to be the jealous type. But if you were already involved, why was I not informed of your relationship in advance before he came aboard?"

"Because we, including my mother, did not want people calling Devlin's appointment into doubt—as you just did." He stood a little taller, ready for the fallout. "What are you going to do?"

"First up, I'm going to stop trying to get him into bed. At least now I know why he was refusing my advances. I'll back off... Does Ambassador Taylor know about us? Humans are a highly emotional species."

He hadn't expected that to be Holjin's response. "Devlin is aware we shared a singular occurrence with no intent on either of our parts to repeat it."

Holjin cleared his throat. "And of the other two?"

"What?"

"Commander Brilli declared your involvement with him and his spouse when they came aboard."

Zal had told Brilli it wasn't strictly necessary to inform Holjin about their shared past as at the time Zal was a guest of his mother and not yet part of the research staff, but Brilli had insisted. "Ours was never a serious attachment in that sense. We're good friends, but no more. And our relationship is no longer sexual and hasn't been for some time. Before he took the post on this ship."

Holjin raised an eyebrow. "Yes, but Chroalians tend to be somewhat demonstrative in their friendships. As you said, Ambassador Taylor has already shown himself to be a credit to this ship, as are you. I don't want him upset, meaning I would have to have you transferred."

The thought hadn't crossed his mind. As far as Zal was concerned, he and Devlin were headed towards bonding, not separation. "He's not the sort of man to overreact. My intention is for him to get to know them, and he'll understand the complexities without there being an issue."

"He's certainly level-headed, but can you really say you know how he will react over a personal matter? You've not known him long, and I daresay there's more you don't know about him than you do."

Holjin might have a general point, but he fundamentally knew Devlin was too good a man to be vindictive over something in his past. "He's aware of our friendship. It's none of your business."

"It will become my business if your relationship is detrimental to my ship."

"It won't be." Holjin might be the captain, but Zal wasn't going to let him intimidate him. They'd technically done nothing wrong, even if they had kept their relationship secret for the sake of Devlin's position. "So unless there was something else you wanted to talk to me about, I'd like to get back to my duties. I have more samples to process than I know what to do with."

"I haven't finished, Lieutenant. If you are in a committed relationship with the ambassador, when are you going to make it known? As it stands, half the ship is looking to bed him. Are you going to keep your temper if someone tries to ensnare him?"

He wanted to say that it was only Holjin's actions that bothered him, but that would lead to questions he couldn't answer: like why he could cope with others wanting his boyfriend but not Holjin. "We had intended the first evening on Xoros to be a starting point, I was going to attend the gala with Devlin, but instead you stepped in, and all of a sudden he was yours."

"That was part of the reason I was concerned when I caught you. But your eyes are glowing pink, Zal. There's no need to be jealous now I am aware of the situation. I would suggest you engineer something for our next away meeting. At least that's a few more days away, and it would be better to convince the general populace that this romance of yours began on ship and not before."

Holjin appeared to want to offer genuine advice, and Zal hadn't expected it. "We'll take your guidance into consideration, sir. But I have to ask, why are you being so helpful?"

"Why wouldn't I be? I want those aboard the *Endeavour* to be happy and fulfilled. I might not like discovering your relationship with Devlin in such a way, but I don't oppose it. I think you pair being together will serve both our species well."

"I…"

Holjin chuckled. "While I don't want to be saddled with a permanent partner, I'm assured many people do, and as long as there is no danger to my ship, I'm happy to see romance blossom."

He had never thought of Holjin in such a way. "Er… thanks."

"I just hope the ensigns learn to back off. I don't want to hear tears and tales of a nasty xenobiologist if you're as grumpy with them as you are with me."

Zal snorted. "Surprisingly, they don't bother me so much. But once they know Devlin's mine, if they continue to pursue him, they'll have more to worry about than a few tears."

Holjin patted him on the shoulder. "Steady now. You were young once."

He laughed. "And I knew not to foist my tail into places where it wasn't wanted."

Chapter Seventeen

Zal had reserved a table in the corner of the officer's mess, and while it was his right to eat in there, he didn't tend to bother, even though the food was better. He thought it would be a nice setting for Devlin to meet Brilli and Appla both as a couple and as his friends. Devlin had taken Scrillia's advice and was meeting with a mix of different people about the ship, and he would come here directly after he'd finished with the chief engineer.

He spotted Brilli's bright pink hair as he entered, and saw Appla had also changed theirs to a violet colour. They were sitting close, and he could see their tails were linked. Brilli's tail was scaly, but Appla's species were furry and Zal had to admit he'd enjoyed the contrast.

"You're early," he said, nuzzling noses with each of them in turn, their standard greeting.

"So are you. Where's your Devlin?" Appla asked.

"He'll be here soon… once Chief Malga has finished with him."

Brilli laughed. "Might as well order some drinks as she can talk someone's tail off."

"Luckily, Devlin doesn't have a tail."

Appla grinned and they wiggled their eyebrows. "But I bet he likes playing with yours."

Devlin's willingness to further explore playing with his tail had been a wonderful surprise, and he would take him up on the offer once they could spend some quality time together and not have to rush. "Mine is a marvellous tail, as you well know. But as far as most people on this ship are aware, I've not gone near him with my tail or any other bit."

"Don't worry, Zal. Tonight you're doing your liaison duties, ensuring Ambassador Taylor gets to know the chief communications officer and his wonderful bond-mate," Appla said with a grin.

The officer's mess was table service, and a white-jacketed waiter glided up to them and handed them the menu of the day.

"Are you still expecting your other guest?" the waiter asked, his tail pointing to the space where Devlin would sit.

"Yes," replied Zal. "He won't be long."

"Can I take a drinks order while you wait?"

Brilli beat him to order. "A bottle of welter wine, please."

Zal groaned as the waiter left. "We should have had the low-alcohol version. You are meant to be giving Devlin the best impression."

Appla stuck out their tongue. It was forked and bright purple. "We will be. You need to relax, Zal. It's not like he's meeting your parents."

"No, he's meeting the two people who I have a 'complicated to explain to a non-Chroalian' relationship with."

Brilli's nostrils flared. "Are you thinking Devlin will have a problem with us? From everything you've said about him, he didn't sound like a stuck-up dilldod."

Zal puffed out his cheeks in exasperation. The last thing he needed was Brilli getting protective. "Of course not. But there's a lot of things we're learning about each other, and since we didn't spend a lot of time talking when we were on Earth, I don't want to worry him about something he doesn't have to."

Appla used their tail to swat Brilli around the head. "Stop it, Brilli. Zal's not a kidlet. He knows what he's doing. And we will behave, but we will be ourselves."

"I wouldn't ask for anything else." He saw Devlin enter the officer's mess. "Here he is."

He waved Devlin over, his stomach doing a little flip at the sight of him in his best suit, meaning Devlin had changed to meet his friends. "Devlin, you've met Brilli, and this is Appla."

Devlin claimed the empty seat. "Zal has told me a lot about you. Pleasure to get to know you."

"Zal's been equally chatty about you," Appla said with a

smirk. "You've most of the ship interested to know more about the new Earth Ambassador."

"I'm sure it's all a matter of me being a novelty. It will soon wear off."

"I heard the betting pool trebled since Sihil intervened... some of the ensigns can get a bit feisty," Brilli said. "But most Chroalians respect a boundary if it's clear."

"Can't say I've witnessed that," Devlin said with a tight smile. "Although I gather from Zal it might be a cultural difference I'll need to adapt to."

"They'll probably still proposition you, but there'll be no real heat behind it." Appla smiled, and although Zal knew they were trying to be friendly, it came out more like a leer. "I'm sure Zal will be more than happy to help see them off."

The waiter reappeared, poured the wine, and confirmed there was no issue with the set menu before leaving. Appla drained their wine in two gulps and motioned to Brilli to top up their glass.

"Are you enjoying life aboard the *Endeavour* so far, Devlin?" Brilli asked, and Zal appreciated his attempt to get the conversation started. There had always been the danger that things would be awkward, and he needed his friends to bring Devlin into the fold.

"Absolutely. I've been working with aliens for over a decade on Earth, but none of it compares to being on an actual spaceship. Every day is going to bring new adventures and challenges, and I can't wait to experience them all. And having Zal assigned to help means the world to me."

"There's a definite sort of person it appeals to. Leaving your home planet is quite something," Appla said.

"The Ambassador Programme is very important to Earth and I was honoured to be chosen." Devlin smiled at Zal. "But there were other benefits. What made you want to leave your home worlds?"

Brilli took a drink of his wine. "I come from a long line of military—so I guess it's in my blood. I've always been good at languages, and once I'd finished studying I signed up for the Exploratory Legion of the Chroalian Space Force."

"I wasn't so noble," Appla said. "I needed a job, didn't fancy becoming a prostitute, which was one of the more interesting of the options I had based on my birth caste, so I set off travelling and worked in various spaceports and bars until I met Brilli."

Zal watched for Devlin's reaction. "I think it's best to follow your heart. It appears to have worked out well for you. How did you meet Zal?"

Zal took a long drink of his wine and hoped Appla would give a censored version. He should have known better because they were not known for watering down anything or being loose with the truth. "I walked in on Zal and Brilli fucking in a club bathroom. Since Brilli was obviously giving good service, I asked to see him after I learnt Zal was only visiting for the weekend."

Brilli cleared his throat. "I've known Zal since our student days. We met in a student bar, and I beat him in a tail-wrestling competition."

"So you dated?" Devlin said, his expression somewhere between confused and surprised.

"No, I told you, there was nothing like that," Zal said quickly. "Friends with benefits is a better description."

"Yeah, and when me and Brilli got together, I got the benefits too," Appla said. Zal had the horrible thought that they believed they were helping. "Zal was travelling regularly and always up for a bit of fun."

Zal knew Devlin would not have missed the fond expression both Appla and Brilli wore. "But you changed to just friends at some point."

"We were open to continuing, but once he started dating Telgan, things changed." Brilli waved his tail at Zal. "Besides which, we were never on the path to making a proper triad."

"I see," Devlin said, but Zal doubted he did. "Was there a reason for that?"

Zal slid his hand onto Devlin's thigh out of sight. "I don't share well if I'm in love with someone romantically. So it was fine with Brilli and Appla because, while I love them as friends, it wasn't more than that."

"Also, me and Appla took our permanency vows and decided we were happy as a couple." Brilli smiled at Appla and tickled them behind their ear with the tip of his tail.

Devlin squeezed his hand but removed it almost immediately as their first course arrived. "This looks... interesting."

The bowls were filled with a bright red liquid. "I don't think you've had these before. It's a speciality of the chef."

Devlin stirred it with his spoon. "What is it?"

"Vegetable soup."

"Not blood?"

"Blood isn't red," Appla said, laughing.

"Mine is," Devlin said.

"Really? Wow! It's just my cum that's red. My blood's green."

Zal choked on his soup. "Devlin didn't need to know that."

"Remember that time you used a dollop as hair gel and then pulled that Filhin on RJ-1 space station?" Appla asked. "We didn't see you for three days, and when you reappeared, you were grinning and shaking."

Devlin had told him that he didn't care about Zal's past, but that didn't mean he'd want to discuss it at dinner. "Appla, this is not a topic for now."

He saw Appla's tail droop and they bit their lip and glanced between Zal and Devlin. "I'm sorry. I'm just a bit nervous. We want Devlin to like us, and I sometimes can't shut up."

Brilli curled his tail around Appla's waist, and Zal felt a pang of loss, knowing Devlin could never do that for him. "Sweetest, I'm sure Devlin understands."

"Of course," Devlin said, quick to answer. "Zal's past sounds a lot more exciting than mine, but it's all part of what makes him who he is today."

"Exactly. We've known Zal for years, so we're not going to

suddenly disappear and not be part of his life. We'll always be there for him and to make sure no one mistreats him."

Zal thought this sounded suspiciously like Brilli trying to give Devlin the warning talk.

Devlin's smile didn't reach his eyes. "I think it's wonderful that Zal has such close friends he can depend on."

The main course arriving allowed Zal to steer the conversation in a less salacious direction, but Appla could find a way to insert a euphemism at any opportunity and while Devlin was doing his best, Zal knew he was getting more uncomfortable at each risqué remark. They speared a ball-shaped confectionary on the end of their fork and waved it. "Hey, Zal, do you remember when you almost had to have your balls pierced? Glad you won that bet—hate to think how long you'd have been out of action if you'd had it done."

"I've not drunk spiro since, nor do I make wagers with strangers any longer."

"Do I want to know what spiro is? Or the bet?" Devlin asked.

"Probably not." Devlin had more than likely heard enough stories for tonight, and it sounded like Zal had spent his younger years fucking anything with a pulse, interspersed with threesomes with his best friends. He'd had fun, but he hadn't been that wild... not really... maybe a little.

Brilli finished his wine. "Sorry to be the adult here, but I've an early shift tomorrow, so I'll need to call it quits. You guys can carry on without me."

"No, it's good," Zal said quickly. "I've a mountain of work to get through and I'm better with a clear head."

"Oh, dear, looks like we've all grown up," Appla said with a pout. "But we should do this again soon."

Devlin nodded. "It's been an experience. Perhaps after Dyun. I've so much to prepare for the conference and not much time."

They left the mess and Brilli gave Zal a hug and Appla did the same, although they petted Zal's neck with their tail and kissed his cheek before waving them off.

The walk back to their corridor was a little awkward, Devlin falling quiet. "Would you like a drink before you retire?" he asked. "I think we might have a couple of things to talk about."

"Yeah, good idea. Something to help me sleep if you have it?"

Once they were inside Zal's cabin, he stepped close to Devlin. "I sense that this evening wasn't that great for you."

"Zal, it's fine. You'd told me you had fun when you were younger. I possibly didn't need some of the details, but I think it's more of a cultural thing."

"They wanted you to like them, and they were trying to be friendly and share their stories with you."

"I get that. I'm going to have to adapt to different ways, and I suppose it's a stark reminder that I've still a lot to learn about you." Devlin bit his lip. "You're good friends, but is it normal for Chroalians to be so close to people not in a romantic relationship? I know I've not been on board long, but most of the crew don't have the same pattern."

"Sometimes, yes. You're getting a distorted image of Chroalia from being on board the *Endeavour*—it's a specific sub-sect of people and what me, Brilli, and Appla, share is pretty common at home, generally speaking, but not so much on a space-ship."

"Makes sense."

"I take it you're not like that on Earth?"

"Many humans have a clear distinction between friends and committed partners, and I'd say that, as a Brit, I'm like my fellow countrymen by being a bit reserved. So bear with me as I learn."

"They're my friends, and I can tone it down a bit." Zal wrapped his arms around Devlin. "But that's all history, and you know it's you I love."

"You don't have to change for me, Zal. We're both going to have to learn each other's ways."

Devlin had tried his best at dinner not to react; he'd not asked Zal to act any differently, and Zal knew that not everyone would be so understanding. His own jealousy over Holjin getting too close to Devlin was making him feel like a hypocrite, and what he really wanted was for Devlin to be secure in the knowledge that it was him Zal loved.

Chapter Eighteen

Devlin pored over the abstracts for the conference on Dyun. While it would be nice not to be the centre of attention like on Xoros, he was a little overwhelmed at the number of potential new species he might meet. Scrillia was listed as a delegate, but Devlin wasn't, and he was relieved that he could try to melt into the background and observe.

"What's wrong?" Zal asked. "You're worrying your bottom lip, and I don't want it so sore that you won't let me kiss you."

"Nothing, not really. The conference on Dyun is a bit daunting, and I'm not sure how to handle it. I don't really have any experience on the topic of diplomacy to share yet."

"They're not expecting you to present, are they?"

"Thankfully not." His invite had been secured last minute by Scrillia and she'd assured him that he would be able to observe, although she expected him to raise questions or to comment from his naïve perspective if asked. "I might have hid under my bed if that had been the case."

"I quite like presenting... if I'm prepared and I know the topic."

"I can't say I'd go as far as I like it, but I can make a credible stab at it. But in this case, I'd have been out of my depth—the topic is on successful interplanetary negotiations."

"Give it time and you will be," Zal said, gracing Devlin with an encouraging smile. "If you're uncomfortable, perhaps you can tag along with me instead. I'm not attending the conference itself, but I'm taking a team down to collect samples."

Zal's offer was nice but not realistic. "I don't think it would look very good if people think I'm hiding. I've been to plenty of these sorts of things on Earth, and I'm hoping my natural schmooze will overcome any reticence."

Zal grimaced. "I hope not, and I didn't even think humans could contract that."

"What?"

"An infectious disease that causes inflammation of the gut, making the individual offload a bilious green sludge from both ends...the schmooze."

"Oh no, not that. It just means to talk well with people and interact in a way that they'll like you. No leaking of anything out of an orifice." Devlin thought he should probably start putting some effort into learning Chroalian and wondered if there was an easy way to check the universal translator for gaps between known words and their meaning in English.

"That is a relief. I was wondering if we just hadn't been together long enough for me to have experienced it."

It was a fair comment and one that needed further assurances. "You'll be glad to know I don't have any cyclic or recurring issues with oozing or otherwise."

"I don't ooze, but I do have a moulting period twice an annual cycle."

"Moulting?" he hoped he'd kept the trepidation out of his voice.

"Of my scales—they'll go dull overnight, and I apply this fancy salt scrub, and the new shiny surface appears." He smiled. "Chroalian couples tend to help each other, sort of a bonding thing."

"I don't have any scales for you to scrub." He felt like he might be missing out on something, and he didn't like the idea.

"I'd noticed." Zal wrinkled his nose. "I suppose if you didn't want to, I could do it myself. Or since Brilli's on board, I could ask him."

Devlin blinked and hoped he'd misunderstood. "Ask him to do what exactly?"

"Er... help scrub my scales."

Zal seemed oblivious to why Devlin might have an issue with another individual, one Zal used to have sex with, helping with such an intimate act. "You know you asked me to tell you things that I would consider inappropriate? Well, that would be one."

"I... oh."

"Only *I* get to scrub your scales from now on, okay?" He'd never in a million years thought he'd get upset over moulting scales. "I consider your scales in the same way you consider my fuzziness."

Zal's eyes went wide as the penny dropped. "Mine."

"Exactly."

Zal crowded up to him. "I'm sorry. I didn't think."

"It's all right. We just have to be clear with each other about where our boundaries are. So that's one of mine, and we don't have to keep going over it. Let's discuss our plans for Dyun."

Zal laced their fingers together, and Devlin could see he was still upset over his misstep. "Does the conference have a reception? I don't have an invite, but if so, then I could be your plus one."

"Not for the first night; might be something after the second day, but I'd have to check. Scrillia said that people will likely meet in smaller groups for dinner, so she thought it wise that I stick with her."

"We could meet after."

Devlin had been thinking along a similar line. "We could make it obvious we were watching the sunset... you know... together."

Zal's tail tickled Devlin's ear. "We will need to make it happen."

"I'm sure the captain and your mum will be more than willing to help."

Zal rested his head on Devlin's shoulder. "I can't wait to wrap my tail around your waist so everyone can see we belong to each other. And to spend the night with you. Honestly, Devlin, I did not realise how hard it would be to have you next door and not be able to sleep curled up around you."

"I want that too."

Zal looked up at him, his eyes starting to turn purple. "You may have noticed I am a very tactile individual."

"I did wonder. I thought your tail was in charge, but aren't you also an individual who is due to go to work?"

Zal glanced over at the time displayed on the wall. "I've gotta go. I've a cycle coming off a temperamental machine, and if they aren't treated correctly, it'll be for nothing."

"And I need to talk to Scrillia to make sure I don't overthink the conference." They shared a kiss and Devlin grinned as he watched Zal leave, his tail swinging. He couldn't wait for Dyun, not because of the conference or meeting new people, but because he would be able to put his arms around Zal and call him his.

*

Zal stared in disbelief at the rack of spoilt samples. So much time wasted, and they had no real idea what had gone wrong, beyond the piece of shit machine that seemed to create a grumpy AI subroutine. He was not in the mood to conduct a root cause analysis, and he called time on the discussion with one of the lab techs, stopping him mid-diatribe about the sequencing machine. "It'll keep for the next shift. We'll talk it through then, and I'm sure a fresh pair of eyes will help to no end."

To be fair, his mood was not helped by Devlin's message saying he was having a drink with Sihil with no hint Zal was invited to join, which was a bit rude as he hadn't wanted to be on his own, so he was delighted when he reached his cabin to find Brilli and Appla heading down the corridor in his direction. "You must've read my mind. I am in need of some company."

He let them into his cabin. "Your Earth boy not about?" Appla asked, their long braid jiggling as they chuckled. "Or have you worn him out?"

Brilli laughed. "I hope you haven't been too rough. You used to get a bit bitey."

"I still do."

Brilli threw himself onto the bed as if he owned the place, and Appla landed next to him. All pretty much what he expected of them. He collected a bottle of a liquor he knew they both liked and three glasses, handing out generous measures before he joined them on the bed, Appla scooting over so they could sit in the middle before putting their head in Zal's lap.

"So all joking aside, how's it going with Devlin?" Appla asked. "He seemed very nice when we met."

"Really well. We've decided that on the next planet, we'll make it look like we got together as a couple. We're planning to watch a sunset on Dyun."

"Oh that's so romantic," Appla said. "It'll be good timing too as there's so many rumours flying around, and surprisingly, you and him as a couple is one I haven't heard."

"Yeah, I heard an ensign say he thought Devlin was having a threesome with Holjin and Sihil."

"He's with Sihil at the moment. He is becoming good friends with her, so I'm not surprised someone started joining the dots."

Appla looked up at him and stroked his belly. "Is everything all right, Zal?"

Brilli pursed his lips. "You're not worried Devlin might do something? I thought you said he was exclusively into men."

"He is. There's nothing but friendship between Sihil and Devlin." He rested his head on Brilli's shoulder. "Devlin has done nothing to suggest he's interested in her. But I wish he'd invited me along this evening."

Brilli nuzzled him with his head, and Zal was glad to receive the affection when he began to play with his hair. "Do you need a proper hug?"

He nodded and found himself moved so he was sandwiched between them, held in Brilli's arms and Appla lying along his back, their three tails linked together.

"What the ever living fuck is going on here?"

Zal scrabbled to sit up as he saw Devlin standing at the bottom of his bed, hands on his hips and a face of thunder.

"It's just a hug," Zal said, confused at Devlin's reaction.

"No, that's you playing Zal in the middle with your exes."

Brilli and Appla rolled away and scrambled off the bed. "We should go."

"Good idea," snapped Devlin.

Zal's confusion was replaced with annoyance as his friends left. "What is wrong with you?"

"Zal, I've just walked in on my boyfriend in a three-way clinch with the couple he used to be in a sexual triad with. How much more comfort were they going to give you?"

"I resent that implication. They are my friends. There was absolutely nothing inappropriate going on. It's no more sexual than what you're doing with Sihil."

"I'm having hand-to-hand combat lessons to ensure my safety. Whereas, I've just walked in on you wrapped up in a puppy pile with two people you were intimately involved with."

Zal tapped his translator, that didn't make sense exactly, but he got the gist. "It was us being friends, nothing more. Don't humans remain friends with their exes?"

Devlin scowled at him. "Not like that."

"I forgot, it's all a bit too affectionate for your species, isn't it?" The words were out before he could stop them, and Devlin looked like he'd been slapped.

"Yes, actually, it is. That sort of connection is for your partner, not your ex-lovers."

"But we've always been like that." Devlin was being unreasonable about his friends. "Even Telgan didn't have a problem with it."

"Your ex-boyfriend was also Chroalian." Devlin huffed. "Why can't you see that I would have a different opinion on the matter? Why can't you understand my point of view?"

"Because it makes no sense."

"You seemed to understand when I said I didn't want Brilli touching your scales."

"That's different. You equated my scales to your fuzziness. I was fully clothed with them just now. Just like you're fully clothed with your combat session with Sihil. There's nothing more behind it."

Devlin shook his head. "You honestly think it's acceptable to get comfort from Brilli and Appla and for me not to be upset? If you want our relationship to work, you're going to have to understand that my boundaries are different to yours, and you'll need to respect them."

He stormed out and Zal was left standing, not believing what had happened. His first instinct was to call Brilli for his insight, but he realised that would upset Devlin even more. He supposed he could talk to his mum, but he had a sneaking feeling she'd agree with Devlin.

Zal poured himself another drink and sat back down on the bed, a waft of Appla's perfume catching him off guard. The fact was they could have been a permanent triad if he'd wanted it a few years ago, but that phase had passed, and now they were two of his best friends. He tried to put himself in Devlin's position, grasp how he'd feel to smell the lingering scent of an ex on Devlin's sheets. His heart plummeted, realising just how out of order this was to Devlin, who had given up everything to be with Zal and who was trying to adapt to a new life. He was going to have to apologise, grovel more likely, and rethink the way he acted with Brilli and Appla.

"Computer, where is Ambassador Taylor?"

"Ambassador Taylor is in his cabin."

Well, at least he hadn't gone far. Another thought dawned on him that Devlin didn't have the support on board ship that he did, and Zal had been dismissive of Devlin's concerns and even made a dig at how humans weren't an emotional species. He hadn't wanted to h'mik Devlin—the humans called it gaslighting for some reason he couldn't figure out. He was fucking this up, and he needed to make things right.

He let himself into Devlin's cabin. Given their current argument, Zal thought Devlin might have locked him out, but he was allowed access as usual. Devlin wasn't in the main room, and he heard the shower running so settled on the bed to wait. His mum would be proud that he hadn't run away from further confrontation.

Devlin emerged dressed in pyjamas, a pair that was one of Zal's favourites as they were slightly too big and hung invitingly low on his hips. He stopped mid-stride, drying his hair.

"Zal."

"I'm sorry," he blurted out.

"What are you apologising for?" Devlin said, huffing, his mood no better despite his shower.

"For being an arsehole."

Devlin's expression was best described as pinched, and he threw his towel over a chair. "Meaning what exactly?"

Zal hated arguments, and he never liked admitting he was the one in the wrong. "For not thinking that the way I acted with my friends might not be appropriate to you."

"Do you even know what I'd think inappropriate or not was with them?"

"I get from your reaction that cuddling together isn't."

Devlin seemed to be fighting an internal conflict. "I don't want to tell you what to do, and if this is something that is fundamental to you and them, I'll do my best not to overreact. But you're going to have to realise it will be difficult for me, at least at the beginning."

Zal hadn't expected this response. He'd seen how upset Devlin had been when he'd found him with his friends, and now he seemed more upset with himself than he had been with Zal, which he didn't understand at all.

"I've known them for years, and it's easier to fall into old habits than make new ones." Devlin's reaction confused him. "I don't want to do anything that hurts you."

Devlin collected a shirt and hid away his fuzziness which made Zal feel even sadder. "We know so little about each other, or how different we are. "

"That will come in time, and we've our whole lives to learn."

Devlin still looked upset. "You said that humans weren't affectionate, and I've not had the greatest dating experience in the past, so I don't want to ruin things. So, am I not loving enough towards you?"

He raced forwards and grabbed Devlin's hand. "Oh no, Devlin. No. You're perfect."

They had such different life experiences. Zal had gone through plenty of lovers in the past, and while Telgan hadn't been the best partner for him, he hadn't been left thinking he was a poor choice. Whereas Devlin had never had a boyfriend who'd realised the wonderful man he was or who had treated him right.

"Do you understand why I'm worried? You're close with your friends and once I calmed down in the shower, I realised I had no right to demand anything of you, and I don't know if I'm ever going to be attentive enough for a Chroalian partner."

Zal's heart clenched. He didn't need Devlin to change. He was the one who had misstepped here, not Devlin. "No, no, no. You're wonderful. I've never been happier."

"But if you're like this with your friends, how much more should I be doing as your lover? I wondered if I've missed something, and maybe it's because you think I've been neglecting you."

Fuck. He was sending all the wrong signals. "I've been jealous over Holjin, and I've not handled my emotions well, but that does not mean you've done anything wrong."

"You've not been bothered by anybody else... It's almost as if you wouldn't mind if something did happen as long as it wasn't with Holjin."

"Like fuck I would. It's not that. I trust you. But Holjin is weird because he's the captain and sexy and a great guy... and I'm being an arse over him because we also have a history." He hated that he'd done this to Devlin and was a little perturbed that Devlin had thought he didn't care. "I know how lucky I am that we got our chance to be together."

"I don't know all your customs, and I know you've had partners in the past that have been important, whereas I've never had that. I'm not asking you to give up your friends either. I would never do that. It's just that the ways you three interact is a bit more intimate than I'm used to."

"You do not have to do all the accommodating here. We're partners, and as such, I need to make an effort not to make you think you're doing something wrong. Which you are most definitely not."

Devlin looked pained and Zal led him over to the bed and pulled him down to lie next to him, face to face. "I love you, and I hate that I can't shout it to the whole ship. Next planet, we'll start our public relationship, and I can't wait for everyone to know that I am the lucky Chroalian who gets to call you theirs."

Devlin's frown disappeared and he reached up and stroked the shell of Zal's ear, which made him shiver in delight. "I'd love that too. I'm sorry for getting angry. I've never cared about anyone as much as you, and seeing you curled up with them made me think the worst."

Zal pulled Devlin into his arms. "There's never been anyone better than you, Devlin. Even the thought of not having you in my life makes me feel sick. We've a lot to learn about each other, and I can't wait to know everything.

Devlin nuzzled into Zal's neck, and Zal stroked his hair. His first instinct was to roll Devlin back and kiss him, but the way he held on tighter made Zal realise Devlin was seeking comfort, not looking for anything sexual. For Chroalians they were generally one and the same, but not for humans, or at least not his human, and Zal was going to need to be more cognizant of Devlin's needs and not just his own. With Telgan it had been easy, both scientists driven by their careers, and it took little to keep them together, and when he'd started to want a deeper connection as part of their relationship, not just the physical side, that's when it started to fall apart. He couldn't imagine that being a problem with Devlin.

"Love you," Devlin murmured. "Stay a bit longer?"

Zal would need to get back to his cabin soon, but he'd wait until Devlin fell asleep before he left. He kissed the top of Devlin's head. "If I could, I would never leave."

Chapter Nineteen

Devlin squirmed in his seat as six pairs and one singular eye stared at him, waiting for his input. To say he had been out of his depth for the majority of the day was being ambitious, and now he was in a smaller group for dinner, he wondered if he could just duck under the table and hide there until he could escape to meet Zal.

"I suppose so. I've not the experience, but it would be very daunting," he managed to finally answer.

Amtu, a cyclops from Riser 4, nodded. "But it could be a mechanism for better outreach. If you were to explain or even demonstrate human physiology to a room of aliens. Perhaps show certain biological processes that might help."

Scrillia retook her seat at the table. "The topic seems to have diverted significantly from before I stepped out."

"I was asking Devlin what he thought of the idea of a sort of show-and-tell about his species." Amtu smiled encouragingly. "He could offer a session to a select group, say of six to eight, and talk them through the way humans work. I imagine audience participation in demonstrating your copulation habits would be very rewarding."

To be fair to the others around the table, they looked as shocked as Scrillia. "Diplomacy comes in many forms, and from my understanding of humans they are unlikely to find that particular option in keeping with their species," Scrillia replied, and Devlin hoped that might be the end of it.

"I don't know. I, for one, would be interested in exploring the idea."

"But you and your people are different in that sense. I mean, you've what, six husbands?"

Amtu preened. "I've just added a seventh." She smiled at Devlin. "With a possibility for an eighth."

Devlin noticed Laya, the individual to his left, shudder. "We Flinns reproduce asexually and physical contact is not something we enjoy," Laya said. "Only the cerebral pursuits are considered worthy."

"That is why it's so important we find a common path," Devlin said. "As you all know, I am on my first steps of this journey, and it is fascinating and rewarding to hear all the different perspectives."

The last of the after-dinner drinks had been consumed, and

Scrillia pointedly placed her napkin on the table. "It has been a long day, and while the workshops have been rewarding and your company this evening even more so, I think we should call it a night. We have another long day tomorrow."

Amtu batted her eye at Devlin. "Perhaps Ambassador Taylor would care to join me for another drink?"

"As much as I would like to accept, I unfortunately have other plans."

"Pity. But we will see each other tomorrow."

"We will have many opportunities to interact." However, he was determined to make sure they were always with other people, because he didn't think Amtu was getting the hint.

Devlin was quick to follow Scrillia out of the private dining room that was part of a conference centre. Several other delegates were finishing up, and as there were many restaurants, bars, and two large hotels, it was busy, including the group of Chroalians from the ship who were hanging out at a bar. He spotted Zal amongst them.

Scrillia winked at him. "I am for my bed, but I am sure Zal would be happy for your company."

He approached the bar, Zal smiling as he got nearer. "Devlin, I thought you'd be busy for a while longer."

The other Chroalians were from the labs, and he hadn't been introduced to them yet. After a quick round of names he didn't think he'd remember later, he declined an offer of a drink. "No, thanks. I was thinking of heading up to one of the lookout points and watching the sunset. I've heard it's very special."

"I'll come with you," Zal said, downing the rest of his drink. He settled the tab with his thumbprint to a terminal on the table. "You lot better not get too drunk. The mudflats we're exploring tomorrow have a smell that does not go well with a hangover."

Relieved that none of the others tried to invite themselves along, they left towards elevators that would take them to the top of the complex. "I hope it won't be too crowded."

"I doubt it. There'll be people about but there's all sorts of special excursions you can book." Zal bit his lip, playing up for the others in the lift. "I could see if there's something we could do tomorrow, if you'd like?"

"Should we ask your colleagues?" Another offer for anyone who might be listening.

"I was thinking it could be just the two of us. If that was all right with you?"

Devlin smiled. "I'd love to."

The lift doors opened and along with the other three occupants of the lift they exited into a lobby for a viewing platform. Zal grabbed his arm and guided him outside. "The best views will be from over here."

Devlin was more than happy to let Zal pull him along, and they emerged onto a balcony overlooking a beautiful, stepped valley. The twin suns were already low in the sky, creating a myriad of colours and an amazing vista that Devlin could honestly say he'd never seen the likes of. "It's stunning."

Zal slipped his hand into his and he turned to look at him. "I've seen a lot of special things in the universe, Devlin, and while this sunset is one of them, it pales into insignificance compared to you."

"Oh, Zal, you're a sweet-talking bastard. But I can't think of a better backdrop for us to share our first public kiss."

They didn't have much of an audience, but there were a few other couples with the same idea, none of whom Devlin recognised. He leant in and brushed his lips to Zal's who pulled him closer. There'd be no mistaking their kiss as a friendly exchange, and Zal's tail came to wrap possessively around Devlin's waist.

"I intend for this kiss to be the first of many," Zal said as he pulled away. "I know we didn't think this through past the kissing tonight, but I would love to take you back to your room."

"It wasn't part of the plan." He stole another kiss. "We talked about having drinks in one of the bars and then out for an excursion."

"Doesn't mean we can't do both." Zal's tail was trying to get under his clothes. "I can be very persuasive."

"I don't want the crew to think I'm an easy target. You wouldn't want them to get the wrong idea and think I'd let anyone have me after a sunset and a bit of chat. Everyone will think they can get a piece of the fuzziness."

Devlin grinned at Zal's low growl. "No. Fuzziness is mine, I will smack the fingers of anyone who tries to pet you."

"Then we should stick to the plan. And aren't you meant to

be sharing a room with someone? Can you go back tonight all loved up and set the scene? Then tomorrow, not come back from our date."

"Why did I have to fall in love with someone so intelligent who talks sense?"

Devlin squeezed Zal's hips. "I tell you what—I promise I will fuck you so thoroughly that it'll make up for not doing it tonight. Then you can return the favour once you've got your breath back."

"Fuck, Devlin. You've made me as hard as a rock. How am I meant to get through the night without you?"

Devlin chuckled. "I'm sure you'll survive."

Chapter Twenty

Zal had returned earlier than expected from exploring the mudflats. A dry spell had left them baked hard, and it wasn't normal for the season, meaning some of the samples he'd wanted weren't available. Returning to his rooms in the hotel mid-afternoon, he killed the few hours before he could meet Devlin by reading. He had a stack of new journals, both published and those sent to him for peer review, but he couldn't concentrate as well as he needed; the plan for the evening kept invading his thoughts and he was looking forward to creating some memories. They were meeting for a drink, then joining a guided tour, which should have a few Chroalians along with them, and Zal hoped seeing him and Devlin together would start the rumours flying. What he really wanted was to shout to anyone who'd listen that Devlin was his.

He'd brought with him an outfit he'd not worn for a while.

The sort of thing his younger self would have strutted around in to get attention, and most times he did. His trousers were cut on the tight side, with his tail free to wave suggestively, matched with a slim-fitting shirt, open and low at the collar, and his dark-red, tempert-beast jacket perfected the look. He'd have never considered himself a true wild child, but he knew he was sending out a certain vibe which he thought Devlin would love.

After applying some of his favourite scent, he headed out to grab a table in a bar that had been recommended. Dyun was an interesting planet, and this city was the capital of the second southern quarter, not as busy as some of the places in the north and made for a more relaxed setting, perfect for the conference Devlin was attending.

He slid onto a stool in the corner of the bar, a glass-and-chrome-type place that looked to attract a wealthy crowd. The waiter wasn't local, his blue skin and the pink ridges on his nose giving him away as a Tumarin. He was cute and knew it, and Zal reckoned he made good tips, especially as he was served quickly and with a smile. When he was younger, he'd have been checking out who was watching him, figuring out who to make eye contact with and who to ignore. But today, even though he'd seen a few individuals throw appreciative glances in his direction, he had no intention of encouraging anyone apart from Devlin.

Zal played a few levels of a game on his info device, looking up frequently. Devlin should be here soon. The last talk he was attending finished a little while ago, and Devlin was going to change and then come meet him. He spotted a couple of Chroalians enter, two of the security ensigns he didn't know well, and take seats in the window. From his recollection of the rota, they weren't recorded as being on the surface, and he wondered why they would be here, as this wasn't a stop marked for general shore leave.

He was replying to a message from Brilli, who hadn't left the ship, when Devlin arrived. As much as he loved Devlin in his suits, this more casual image made him almost knock over his drink. Tailored trousers paired with a dark red shirt gave Devlin a suave look, and Zal wanted to lick him from head to toe.

He took a picture of Devlin as he spotted Zal and smiled. Zal thought he was the luckiest bastard in the universe. He sent it to Brilli.

ZAL: *How jealous will the rest of the crew be knowing he's mine?*

BRILLI: *If I weren't bonded, and he was single, then I'd be someone else after him... I'd watch your tail if I were you.*

Zal didn't get the chance to reply as Devlin was sliding onto the seat next to him. His first instinct was to kiss him, but he wasn't sure he could stop if he started.

"You look amazing," Devlin said. He leant in close and pressed a kiss to his cheek.

Zal's tail, which often had a mind of its own, slid around

Devlin's waist. Any Chroalian watching couldn't miss the significance. "I must say you're as attractive out of a suit as in one."

"I've been thinking a lot about yesterday evening. I was worried you might not want to kiss me again."

"I want to do far more than kiss you."

Devlin smirked but the cute waiter reappearing prevented him from saying anything, and Devlin ordered the same drink as Zal. "It's an acquired taste," Zal warned as the red famaco was placed in front of Devlin. "But it's supposed to add an extra special taste to other activities...if you know what I mean."

"I can't say I've any complaints about how Chroalian jizz tastes."

"Jizz? You don't call your mittis jizz! That sounds disgusting. Like something infected."

Devlin laughed. "I won't be calling it that any more. But, so far, I like the Chroalian version. Although I have only a very small sample size to go by."

Zal poked him with the point of his tail and grinned. "If you know what's good for you, it'll remain that way. You're not conducting a statistical analysis; there's no additional variables you need to consider."

Devlin had been confused that Zal had seemed unbothered by the rest of the crew's attraction to him, and he thought the odd comment in the right vein wouldn't hurt even though he trusted Devlin completely.

"Good job I found perfection on my first attempt."

"I knew you were clever." Zal picked up his glass. "Here's to your continuing mission to build relationships with non-humans. I think you'll need to allow time for extra study with me. Oh, say a lifetime or so—just to make sure we cover all the areas."

Devlin's eyes went wide as he took a sip of his drink. "Bloody hell. I can't tell if that's super strong in taste or alcohol."

"Bit of both. I'm not sure if your human constitution is up for more than one of them, and it might be good to get you a glass of water in case you need it."

It was as if the waiter had read his mind, as he glided up with a carafe of water and two glasses. "That's a house special blend. Best to keep hydrated if you want to make sure you have a good rest of the night," he said with a wink as he left.

He poured Devlin a glass of water. "Drink up. I do not want you incapacitated for what I have planned for later."

Devlin dutifully drank his water. "I'd hate to be the reason Earthmen got the reputation of being lousy lovers."

"Oh, there is no chance of that. Mind you, if a rumour were to circulate of such a nature then maybe I wouldn't have to contend with all your wannabe suitors."

"But that would mean you're happy with a poor lover, so what would that say about you?"

Chroalians were known as a friendly race, and there's no way he'd be expected to put up with someone who couldn't satisfy his needs if his lover were able, so he would be thought of as the same. "I'd much prefer them looking on enviously, knowing you were mine and they couldn't have you."

Devlin took his hand and threaded their fingers together. From the corner of his eye, Zal saw a few ensigns from the ship had entered the bar, and they had seen them. One wasn't being subtle, craning her neck to get a good view. Perfect.

"We should make a move. The transport won't wait for us," Zal said, kissing Devlin's knuckles. With a bit of luck, the ensigns would already be spreading the gossip via their communicators about the cosy little drink he'd shared with Devlin.

They left the bar hand in hand, Zal wrapping his tail around Devlin's waist. The gesture might be a touch too much on the intimate side for a first date, but Zal decided better to clearly show his intent rather than someone interpreting his actions as just being friendly to his charge.

The meeting point for the tour wasn't far, on the edge of the conference compound, and around twenty others were already congregating as they arrived. Zal tutted as he saw his mum was waiting there, standing with who he thought might be ambassadors of three other species. She looked as surprised as he did.

Her three companions looked delighted to see Devlin and the female cyclops waved at him. "Devlin, lovely to see you. Our paths didn't cross today."

"Zal, I wasn't aware we were taking the same tour. I would have chosen another."

"I'm surprised you're doing a tour... I thought you'd seen most of what Dyun has to offer in this area."

"Ambassador Amtu invited me," Scrillia said, gesturing to the cyclops on her left. "Since I didn't have plans for the evening, I accepted. If you'd prefer, I could head back to the hotel."

Amtu looked confused. "Why would you do that?"

"Zal is my son. I think he hoped to spend the evening with Devlin."

"Now we all can."

Scrillia patted her arm. "A young man would not want his mother along on a date with a new boyfriend."

Amtu's eye widened. "Oh!"

Zal wouldn't send her away. Part of her job was to strengthen ties with other ambassadors, and these sorts of excursions were great for that. "Don't be silly. You're welcome to stay."

Scrillia smiled. "I'm sure we can sit at the back, out of your way."

A land-based people-carrier drew up. This was not how he was hoping his date with Devlin would go, but it could have been worse. His mum liked Devlin, so at least he knew she wouldn't deliberately try to sabotage their date.

Chapter Twenty-One

Devlin could understand Zal's frustration, but Scrillia had offered not to come and Zal had told her it was fine, so now they would just have to make the best of it. They claimed seats away from her and the other ambassadors who were at the rear of the bus on what was meant to be a short trip out into the shrub. He had expected them to move a little faster as there was no tour guide on the bus to give commentary, so no reason to travel at such a sedate pace. The average London tourist would be complaining by now.

There were a couple of Chroalians in the group, and Devlin recognised other species from the people he'd met over the last couple of days but no one there individually, which meant they wouldn't be drawn into small talk.

"It is kind of funny if you think about it," he said, hoping to get Zal to lighten up. "We'll be able to tell the story about how your mum gatecrashed our first official date."

"I don't see how breaking a fence would add a humorous spin to it, Devlin."

Another term lost in translation. "But at least we're here—together and in public. We were never going to do anything too risqué, and we can still have a kiss and a cuddle."

"I suppose you do have a point, but it does feel a bit like having a chaperone."

"I am dating a Chroalian, so someone has to protect my virtue."

Zal snorted. "Bit late for that."

They were slowing further and Devlin could see no reason for it from where he was sitting. He nudged Zal. "Any idea why we're moving so slowly? Am I missing something?"

Zal shrugged. "I just assumed the terrain was poor."

Devlin stared out the window. The vehicle had caterpillar tracks and the land didn't appear overtly rugged. "I don't think it's that."

"Maybe it's how they do things here. We've loads of time before the sunset, so there's no need to race anywhere."

Devlin had been in too many odd situations to explain this away so easily. A voice crackled over the intercom. "Guests, we are experiencing some minor mechanical issues. Please bear with us as we reduce our speed further to run a series of diagnostic routines."

"See, there's your answer."

Devlin wasn't convinced. "Surely they would have conducted a check before we left. How likely is it that the vehicle is suddenly struck by issues?"

"More than you think. Some of my lab equipment breaks down on a whim."

"But you're not taking people out into the middle of nowhere." His gut wasn't keeping quiet over this, and he didn't think Zal should be so blasé. "I'd expect there should be strict safety protocols. This is an advanced civilisation after all."

"Devlin, you worry far too much."

Devlin saw several figures appear, seemingly out of nowhere running alongside the transporter. There was something about their build that was familiar, and Devlin stood to get a better look.

"What are you doing?" Zal asked.

"Something's going on. I'm sure of it." He didn't have a weapon; he'd been told he didn't need one since the place wasn't a threat, and there would be security on hand if needed. Well, he needed security now, and there wasn't a sniff of it about. He glanced around and from his initial assessment, none of his fellow passengers were obviously armed.

No one else seemed to be concerned, the light chatter benign and on the edge of annoying. Were people really so blinkered to their surroundings?

Zal tugged at his sleeve. "Devlin, sit down. We'll be on our way any moment; you'll see."

Zal wasn't military; he might carry the lieutenant rank, but it was honorary. He hadn't gone through the training, and it showed. "I'll be straight back. Stay in your seat."

"Devlin?"

He walked along the central aisle, towards an emergency exit near the back where Scrillia and the other ambassadors were sat. The men outside were still keeping up with the transporter, and a flash of blond hair and pointy ears made his stomach drop. He'd remember the species that had boarded the *Endeavour* anywhere, and they were real, and were now here. It couldn't be a coincidence.

More people were standing up, getting in his way as he tried to push past them and get to the back of the bus. He heard a scream as the back door was wrenched open and Scrillia toppled backwards.

Devlin shoved his way through the other passengers, now also trying to see what was going on, and he had to use a couple of shoulder barges to get his point across. The other ambassadors with Scrillia were huddled together for safety in the opposite corner of the transporter. He could hear scuffles from outside, unsurprising as he didn't expect Scrillia not to put up a fight. His training kicked in, knowing how dangerous a hostage situation could get, and with little information about the hostiles, he knew he had to be careful, but he couldn't afford to hesitate.

He saw Scrillia struggling outside with one of the "space elves" as it grabbed her by the hair. He really should have found a better name for them, but it would do for now until they identified their species. His three compatriots were scouting ahead, and Devlin noticed they were armed with what looked like disruptors. He only hoped they weren't set to kill.

Devlin only had one opportunity to use surprise to his advantage, but if he could disarm one, he could use the bastard's weapon against the others. He rushed forward and lunged at the blond who had hold of Scrillia, knocking him off balance and to the ground. Devlin's sharp punches to his pointy features were enough to stun him, and Devlin grabbed his gun. "Get back in the transporter," he ordered Scrillia.

He checked the settings on the gun, surprised to see it was the same manufacturer as those used by the Chroalians. It could be a coincidence, but there couldn't be that many arms manufacturers, and something wasn't adding up here. With two taps to the top of the barrel, he reduced the settings to lower stun and fired off several volleys in the direction of the now-retreating attackers. Two of them dropped to their knees. He'd always been a good shot, but then all three of them disappeared into transporter beams and were gone. He turned back to the fourth, who was sitting up and reaching for his communicator.

Devlin snatched it from his chest, threw it to the ground and stamped on it. He tried to get to his feet, but Devlin smacked him across the side of his head with the weapon, knocking him out.

He went over to Scrillia, who had ignored his request and had not returned to the bus. She was as stubborn as her son.

"You really are kind of wonderful, aren't you?" Scrillia said with a smile, not looking at all concerned that she'd nearly been kidnapped.

Zal came out and leant over them. "Mum, are you all right? What's going on?"

Devlin stared at Scrillia and then at the unconscious lone offender he'd knocked out, his friends long gone. "I'd like to know too," Devlin said.

He stood and offered Scrillia his hand which she took. "I'll explain when we're on the ship," Scrilla said. "But you've nothing to worry about."

"I'll be the judge of that."

All the things that had happened—the boarding that never was, his transporter incident, being taken to one side by Filote, and now this kidnapping—were all beginning to sound like a series of elaborate ruses, and Devlin did not like being taken for a fool.

Her communicator beeped, and she tapped it to answer. "Scrillia."

"Report." He recognised Holjin's voice.

"As expected. Can you lock onto me, Zal, and Ambassador Taylor and beam us aboard?"

"Ready when you are."

"Three to beam up, Captain."

Before Devlin could question further, he was back in the ship's transporter bay. Holjin and Dr Golic were waiting. "Dr Golic would like to examine Devlin to confirm he wasn't hurt in the altercation."

"No one is doing anything until someone tells me what's going on," Devlin insisted. Zal looked confused and Holjin impressed.

"I think you've probably got your own suspicions, and knowing you, they'll be correct," Holjin said, smirking.

"Why did you try to stage the kidnapping of Ambassador Scrillia?" It hadn't been a well-thought-out attempt, but he'd give them marks for trying. "And who was the pointy-eared bastard whose face I bruised with my fist?"

"Devlin, what are you talking about?" asked Zal.

At least Zal wasn't party to whatever was going on, as he didn't know if he could get over those sorts of trust issues. "I'd like a full explanation myself, rather than rely on my own conjecture."

"Please let Dr Golic do a brief examination, and then we'll take this conversation somewhere private," Holjin said. "Lieutenant Catenmir can come with us. He might as well hear everything firsthand."

"I'd only tell him anyway," Devlin said, unrepentant.

"My point exactly."

"Tell me what?" demanded Zal. "And what's all this about a staged kidnapping?"

Devlin took his hand. "I think we're going to get answers to some of our questions. But I'm not sure either of us are going to like them very much."

Golic stepped forward and Devlin didn't stop him from

conducting a scan. He had a slight twinge in his hand from the punches but nothing else. From his medical case, Golic removed something that looked like a small pen. "This will reduce the inflammation in your hand and deal with any pain. If you've any stiffness or increased discomfort, come straight to Medbay."

He placed the device to the underside of Devlin's wrist, and he felt nothing more than a slight pressure, followed by a warming sensation, and the ache disappearing.

Holjin was already heading down the corridor. "Come on, then."

Zal scowled and his tail trembled. "Devlin, I don't know what's going on, but I won't let them split us up."

Scrillia squeezed his arm. "There's no danger of that, my darling."

Devlin knew he should not start overthinking things; he'd get answers within a few minutes, but his brain wasn't the sort to stand down, and he couldn't help but come to the conclusion that the Chroalians themselves were behind the happenings, although he was still postulating the reasons why.

Once inside Holjin's ready room, Devlin and Zal joined Scrillia on the sofa while Holjin remained standing. "So, Devlin, I'm sure you've figured out what's been going on."

"You've been testing me." He was pretty sure that was the case. "The fake space elves boarding the ship, the warning about the council, even the transporter incident, all to see how I'd react. Then the kidnapping, and there you were sloppy—using the same pretend species was amateurish."

Zal was staring with his mouth open, looking cute but gorm-less. "But, Devlin, why would anyone want to test you? You were chosen as Earth Ambassador and accepted aboard; that should have been enough."

Diplomacy didn't work like that, and in the back of Devlin's mind, it had always been a bit too easy that the Chroalians had been so welcoming. He'd ignored the niggling feeling, because of his link to Zal, and that Ambassador Scrillia had the sort of influ-ence that made things go away, but he'd been naïve.

"I don't think this is specifically about me, Zal. I reckon any-one who'd taken the role would have been subjected to the same."

Holjin nodded. "We were already in negotiations about the ambassador programme, but several members of the UoP didn't think humans were ready. We noted there were ways and means to judge that. Scrillia said there would be opportunities to allow us to make a further assessment once you were on board. Once I learnt about your relationship, it was obvious why she had changed her position to support the Earth's venture."

"The only way I could get the council's permission to ratify Earth's Ambassador Programme was to agree to a number of measures, including seeing if the new ambassador was up to the job," Scrillia explained. "I had no doubt of your capability and em-pathy, Devlin—your work on Earth spoke for itself—but there's more to being an ambassador than not causing trouble. Solving issues and spotting problems are important too."

232 | Rebecca Cohen

"So you had me running hundreds of samples of nothing just to test Devlin," Zal said, incensed.

Typical Zal would cotton on to that part. "To be honest, Zal, I thought you'd be more concerned about making the crew believe a threat of being boarded. Or that the same unknown race had tracked down and pretended to kidnap your mother."

Zal shrugged. "I suppose so. But now I know they weren't real, I've still got a backlog of real work."

"I've a seasoned crew on the *Endeavour*," said Holjin. "They weren't going to panic over this, so if anything, it was an excellent training exercise."

"Who else knew?" Devlin hoped not too many because, as much as he could understand the need to make sure he was up to the job, it would be hard to trust a whole crew of people who'd been out to see if he would fail.

"Dr Golic, Commander Brilli, Commander Crins, and a few of his men—including two security ensigns who were sent to the planet to keep an eye out on Dyun. No more than a handful on board, plus a few at high command and the UoP Security Council."

"Brilli knew?" gasped Zal.

"As chief communications officer, he had to be told," Holjin said.

"But... I..."

"He might be one of your best friends, Zal, but his duty is first to his ship," Devlin said. "But I imagine him being your friend meant he could monitor for issues between us since he knew of our relationship."

It dawned on Devlin that if Brilli was in on the scheme, and he knew about his and Zal's relationship, he'd either withheld the information, or Holjin had known too. "How long have you known about me and Zal?"

Scrillia cleared her throat. "From the beginning. As the captain, I had to tell him."

Zal looked scandalised. "You knew, and you still pursued him?"

Again, trust Zal not to get the bigger picture here.

"Yes, but it was all for show. I agreed to play along, but I have principles that I do not chase after people who are attached and was not particularly happy to do so. Put it this way, Zal, if I'd succeeded, you'd have been better off without him."

"Holjin and I agreed that he would discover you on Dyun," Scrillia explained. "But he caught you on Xoros and couldn't ignore the situation."

"But he pretended to be Devlin's new partner on Xoros. He could've backed off then." Zal sounded hurt. "There was no need for him to do that."

"Zal, you have to understand that there is more to this than your feelings," Scrillia said, sounding a little exasperated. "Holjin was protecting Devlin from some unwanted attention. In the long run, there has been no damage to your relationship with Devlin. On the contrary, you could even use the situation to your advantage, saying Holjin's actions triggered you to make a move for

Devlin's affection."

"There's still the question of whether I passed." Devlin looked at Holjin. "I don't blame you for needing to know my capabilities, but I don't want to be sent back to Earth."

"There's no danger of that, Devlin. You've shown you've a brilliant mind for strategy and you're adaptable." Holjin clapped him on the shoulder. "You're also brave, but not in a foolhardy way. Earth is very lucky to have you as their ambassador, and I consider myself blessed to have you on the *Endeavour*."

He was relieved to hear Holjin's position, even if he was still pissed off. "Thank you."

"Just a pity Zal managed to wrap his tail around you first, as I'd have loved to have had you in other ways too."

Holjin sniggered as Zal growled and Scrillia laughed. Devlin still had questions. "So am I considered fully acceptable now or should I expect more?"

"It's done. I need to make my report, but as far as I'm concerned you're a worthy candidate, and if you're open to the idea, I would like to invite you to join some of my senior crew meetings. Not all of them, but I do think you'll add an extra dimension."

Zal was clearly agitated. Devlin could tell from the way his tail flicked that he was not happy with the situation. He put himself in Zal's shoes, learning his mother and best friend were in on a secret plot to test his lover was an obvious shock, and Devlin would need to support him. Holjin's reassurance the trials were over was enough for Devlin, and knowing it was done in the best interests of the ship and his positive action would only benefit Earth's intent, he would be able to put this to one side. Zal, not so much.

"I must admit I am intrigued about how you carried out your tests. It can't have been easy to create the space elves with enough verisimilitude to deceive your own crew. And the transporter."

"*Space elves*? That's a new one on me, but I'd be happy to provide you with the technical details, but I want to assure you that you were never in any real danger."

Scrillia snorted. "Not at the hands of the crew, but you don't know how you'll be received by the other species we visit. But you did demonstrate on Dyun that you're more than able to protect yourself. Sihil will be impressed."

"Did she know?" Devlin asked. He'd assumed not, but he had to be sure.

"No, but I will inform her directly after we've finished." Holjin chuckled. "She'll be livid she wasn't in on it, but then proud you pulled off stopping a kidnapping."

"It wasn't real."

"You weren't to know that."

Holjin walked over to one of the screens and tapped it several times. "I've transferred the information I can share of the details of the plan. There are some things not even I'm party to, including who issued the final orders, but I'm doing this to show you have no reason not to trust me."

Devlin stood. "I want to digest this a little. Maybe talk things through with Zal. My biggest fear once I guessed what you were up to was you'd return me to Earth, but as that's no longer your intent—"

"It was never our intent," Holjin added. "Re-education and training would have been the first steps. The Chroalians aren't going to let you fail on your first attempt. We have to consider our own reputation, and that will mean you do not get to fail your mission or run home telling tales."

"I'm not the sort of person to tell tales or be sent away easily."

Holjin grinned. "And that's exactly why you're here, Devlin."

Chapter Twenty-Two

Zal lay with his head on Devlin's belly, enjoying the way Devlin ghosted his fingers across the scales on Zal's lower back. He should have been celebrating news of their involvement spreading through the crew. He'd had plans for them to wander into the mess hand in hand and stare down anyone who dared covet his Devlin. There was no reason why they still couldn't. In fact, Devlin's swift actions in rescuing Ambassador Scrillia would have made it even more perfect if it weren't for the machinations behind the incident.

"It's okay for you to be upset, Zal. Hearing people have kept things from you, even for all the right reasons, isn't nice."

He knew Devlin would understand. "I've always known my mum has to keep secrets. I just didn't expect them to affect me."

"Put it this way—if she hadn't done so, I probably wouldn't

be here. So some things are worth the cost. I don't particularly like being tested, but if it is what's needed to be the ambassador and to be with you, then they can do it as often as they like."

Devlin said all the right things, and if he was being honest with himself he knew Devlin was right, but it wasn't only his mum, but Brilli too.

"I'm also a little weirded out at Brilli knowing."

"That's a different issue. He's your friend, someone you've been more than friends with, and you've no doubt told him or he knows things about you you'd have never told your mum."

"I don't like the idea that he could have been feeding things back I've told him about us." Like a spy. "I wonder if Appla knew as well."

"You need to talk to him, see if he'll tell you if he did pass anything along. It's a trust issue between the two of you, and you shouldn't let it fester, but I don't believe he'd have told his spouse as it seems to have been a closely ring-fenced operation. I know I wouldn't have been allowed to if I were in a similar position."

"You're right. I don't even know if he's been told we now know."

"Then you should speak to him as soon as you can. You can check if he's on duty."

Zal sat up. Devlin could have easily used this to his own advantage to get Zal to put more distance between Zal and his friends, their shared past making things a little tricky, but once again Devlin showed Zal just how good a man he was, trying to get him to make peace with his troubles.

Part of Zal thought he should stay with Devlin, but until he spoke with Brilli he'd be churning this through his mind, unable to settle. "I think he's on first shift today. Would you mind if I went now? This can't have been easy for you either."

Devlin cupped his cheek and kissed him. "Of course not. You need to do this. For me, on reflection, I should have expected it. Knowing safeguards are in place isn't a bad thing. If it had continued, or I'd found out later, then I think I'd have had more of a problem."

"Or if I'd been involved."

Devlin pursed his lips. "I'll be honest, if you'd been involved, I'm not sure we'd be having this sort of conversation. I need to trust my partner, and hiding this level of secret, where I was directly impacted, would have been disastrous for that."

Zal nodded, likely feeling the same way. "I don't think I could keep those things from you. We should probably talk to my mum about what you are allowed to share with me. But I would hope anything that would affect each other directly would be allowed."

"The Ministry back on Earth had levels of clearance based on how long a couple had been together, but that was different. Someone knowing generally about the existence of aliens compared to direct information about an individual is a completely different kettle of fish."

"Fish? Are they boiled?" he asked, having no clue where Devlin was going with this.

Devlin chuckled, his expression so fond it made Zal want to hold him tight. "Sorry. Another silly Earth saying."

They shared a kiss, and Devlin reassured him again that he didn't mind him going, and after checking with the computer for Brilli's location, Zal went off to Brilli's cabin.

He waited for Brilli to answer, and he still wasn't sure what he would say. Brilli had a duty and he had to do that whether he was Zal's friend or not. The door slid open and Brilli stood there. "Holjin told me the exercise was over and you knew. I've been expecting you."

Zal had known Brilli for years and never had he felt such distance between them. He accepted a drink of a sweet liquor they both enjoyed and took a seat by the porthole. "I'm not here to throw accusations around. I just want the truth about your involvement and what you told your superiors about me and Devlin."

Brilli stretched out his legs in front of him and sighed. "Holjin knew you were a couple, so it's not like I broke a trust. We were running test cases to assess Devlin's abilities to see if he had the potential to fulfil his role as needed. I monitored his communications but only pertinent information was passed on."

"Such as?"

"Nothing about you. More Devlin's ability to draw conclusions, to identify the important things to research, how he didn't get sidetracked." Brilli leant forward. "I said nothing about your niggles or arguments over me and Appla. I only would have mentioned anything if there was a threat to the ship—and there wasn't."

"Does Appla know?"

Brilli shook his head. "No. There was no need to tell them. But I had a duty to report anything of concern. It's the same duty you have to ensure the safety of the ship and our species. If Appla started doing something that could hurt the Chroalians I'd report them, as you would Devlin. It's one of the things you have to consider when in an interspecies relationship in our type of work."

Zal hadn't thought about it like that, but then Brilli was right. Thankfully, he believed Devlin would never put him in that position. "Okay."

"I swear I didn't pass on anything you'd entrusted to me about your relationship with Devlin. I admit I did have my own worries about you having your tail turned so fast by a pretty alien, but now I've met Devlin I can see why."

"You didn't say anything. Given how quickly things happened between you and Appla, that's somewhat hypocritical."

"Appla's different. They'd been away from their own planet for years when we met, and this is Devlin's first chance to leave his home and he did so to be with you after such a short time."

"That should work in his favour, not against."

"Come on, Zal. I'm not saying he wasn't a good choice, just that I was cautious. You mean a lot to me and Appla. We want to see you happy. You couldn't find that happiness with us, or Telgan, but I can see that Devlin has given you such a resounding sense of joy I've never seen you experience before—I'd never do anything to ruin that, but I still had a duty to do."

"I understand. But do you understand why I'm upset?"

"Of course. I'm glad you came to see me, and that we could discuss it rather than you hiding and me having to drag you out."

He'd done that before after he'd called it complete quits on sleeping with Brilli and Appla. "Devlin said I should talk to you."

"Then he's a better person than most. Our relationship has to look strange to Devlin, so him being willing to support us continuing to be close friends can't be underestimated." He grinned. "When are you going to start courting him properly? Half the ship's talking about you fucking the human."

"Are they saying that's all there is to it? I don't want the pipe cleaners and duct dusters thinking they can win him off me."

"Bit of a mix..."

Zal knew he didn't have any competition, but he would like to make sure his intentions were clear. "He's mine."

Brilli chuckled. "So, soon on the courtship front, then."

*

Devlin had received a message from Sihil, and with Zal hopefully rebuilding bridges with Brilli, he decided to accept the offer to meet her for a drink in the officer's mess. He may have thought twice if it was in the main canteen, not wanting to be under the full scrutiny of the ship's eager ensigns, who he was sure would not be put off by the rumour he and Zal were together.

She was already seated when he arrived, and she waved her tail at him as he approached. A Chroalian's tail was a wonderful part of their anatomy, so expressive, and he was learning to read an individual's tail's quirks. "I've a bottle of kirsha coming. I thought we could celebrate."

"Celebrate what?" he asked with a smirk as he sat.

"You being as marvellous as I've been telling the captain you are. I'm a bit annoyed I wasn't allowed to be in on the secret Devlin-testing missions. I would have probably pushed you harder."

"You know, I'm quite relieved you weren't. I'd hate to think you'd become my friend solely for monitoring purposes."

A silver bottle arrived, and Devlin had no idea what it was, beyond shiny-looking. "It might have made it odd. But now Holjin is talking about making you an honorary member of the senior crew, which means I can rope you into all sorts of things."

"I do have a job of my own and Zal to spend time with."

Her grin was positively filthy. "Oh yes, that's another thing to celebrate... So, tell me, how are you liking Chroalian physiology?"

"Let's just say I'm very appreciative of scales and tails."

She waved her tail at him. "I bet you are, and he's bound to get all sorts of questions about humans being hairy. Tell me... are you?"

"Some of us are. I have a decent covering that Zal seems to like."

She snorted and poured them a glass each of a fizzy red liquid. "This is a traditional drink from the region I'm from on Chroalia."

"I'm honoured you wish to share it with me." Devlin picked up his glass and held it out for a toast.

"To the further adventures of Devlin Taylor, Earth Ambassador extraordinaire."

Chapter Twenty-Three

Talking to Brilli had been one thing, but he also needed to speak to his mum. He'd been used to her not being able to share aspects of her work, but this was far more personal, and he wished she'd at least hinted at what was going on.

Scrillia stared at him over the rim of her cup. "There's no need to be so upset over this, Zal. You have what you wanted, which is Devlin, and you're going to get to keep him."

"I didn't think there was any danger of me not getting to keep him."

She sighed. "Zal, love blinds us. You wanted Devlin back, and you got him, but if you'd been thinking about the wider consequences, you'd have realised that Devlin would have had to demonstrate he was worthy."

Zal wasn't naïve; he'd known that, but it was the way they

had gone about having Devlin prove himself he didn't like. "He would have done so through his diplomatic duty. The farce of creating a fake boarding party with made-up aliens is embarrassing. Were you also behind Filote warning Devlin about the potential danger to Earth?"

"She believed what she said. We merely engineered the situation so she had the opportunity to tell Devlin. We needed to see how he might react and use the information. His actions were very telling: he didn't lose his head and did pretty much what I would have done in a similar situation. I lost that bet to your father."

"Dad knows about this? Why did he get to be told and not me? Surely he doesn't get to have such privilege because he's your spouse."

She carefully put down her cup and stared at him. "I thought you were aware of your father's occupation."

As far as Zal was concerned Dharl's job was supporting his mum. "He's your husband."

She cleared her throat, looking uncomfortable. "Evidently not. Zal, I know we never discuss my work directly, but you must have realised most ambassadors tend not to travel with their family, especially after the children have reached an age of independence?"

He'd never really thought about it. His career had been in research and not linked to his mother's travels before joining the *Endeavour*. He would visit regularly if she was in the vicinity of his work and vice versa but had thought his father was there for company.

"Er... no."

"Your father had, or rather has, a role in military intelligence. He's a member of the Sentinel League."

Zal dropped his cup. The Sentinel League was known for covert operations or protecting senior officials and were part of an elite squad supporting the maintenance of the accords, including dealing with undesirables. "He's your bodyguard?"

Scrillia handed him a tissue to mop up the tea. "More like he's there to ensure the mission and engagements I'm on are safe. Not security in the physical sense. Dharl's a strategist."

He had no real clue what that meant beyond his dad being connected to people Zal didn't know existed. If Dharl was on board the *Endeavour* in that capacity then he had an obvious question. "Was he involved with the tests for Devlin?"

"Yes. He helped plan most of them. But he also knew that Devlin was a good man. Dharl was convinced that Devlin was the best human for the job. He devised the tests to showcase Devlin's diverse skills."

"He rigged them?"

Scrillia tutted. "Zal, you're an intelligent man; are you really suggesting your father would do something so silly?"

"But you said he picked the tests."

"Yes, he read Devlin's service record provided by the Ministry and used Devlin's past experiences to challenge him in areas he should be successful at if he was as good as the humans said he was. It meant he would succeed if it was true…and it was."

"I think I'm more confused than ever."

She looked at him fondly. "The Ministry justified Devlin's appointment based on his past career experience. There were incidents of dealing with rogue aliens, portal misuse, and kidnapping. All of which Dharl mimicked with his tests. If Devlin couldn't cope with them, his record must have been falsified, and he'd have failed."

"But if he had failed, surely there was a risk he'd have been sent home, and I'd have lost him." He didn't even like thinking about that possibility.

"Then he wouldn't have been the man you fell for. Nevertheless, he would have been given another chance. Holjin talked of helping and training, and he wasn't lying. Although I don't think I'd have been able to stand by and watch you fall further in love with a man who wasn't who he said he was."

"Devlin's perfect for me."

"I agree. But that's because he's who he claims to be. Not a liar, a cheat, or someone taking shortcuts. But the wonderful Devlin Taylor. He is quite special."

Zal had a lot to process. His father wasn't a companion to his mother, and if he thought about it properly there had been signs. But he'd also set Devlin up to win at the tests, which at the same time would have exposed him if he'd failed. It was a brilliant strategy and showed why Dharl was a member of the Sentinel League. "I should talk to him. Dad, I mean."

"Let me speak to him first. We were under the impression you knew, not all the details, but at least a general idea of what Dharl does." She laughed. "I don't know if he'd be impressed by his own acting skills that his son didn't realise, or appalled you thought him my equivalent of carry-on luggage."

Chapter Twenty-Four

Devlin sat quietly for several seconds after Zal had finished explaining about Dharl's involvement in the Chroalian subterfuge. Zal's father was a nice man, understated and pleasant with every interaction he'd had with Devlin. At no point had his future father-in-law struck him as someone who would be in charge of important strategic operations, but then other people had said the same about him.

"Are you all right?" he asked Zal, sitting in Devlin's cabin. "You've had a bit of a shock."

"I think so. It's not the strangest or worst thing you can find out about your parents, but I'm feeling a bit stupid for not realising."

"How much does anyone know about their parents? It's a specific relationship and balanced with nuances that change over time. The protector you remember who kept you safe as a child is different to the one getting in your way as a teen and then trying to understand you as an adult."

"I thought I knew him well enough but now it feels like I don't and it's odd."

"Perhaps there's something you can do together to rebuild your bond. I don't know him well enough to suggest anything, and I can't say I had the chance to do anything with my parents." He'd never known his mother, and his father had been a shell of a man. Devlin thought Zal was lucky to have the parents he did and the opportunity to be with them so much as an adult, able to get to know them beyond being Mum and Dad.

"Oh, Devlin, I'm sorry for being so insensitive. Here's me wittering on, when you've suffered much more than I have."

"You don't have to apologise. But you've the chance to make sure this doesn't come between you, please don't miss out on that." He'd make sure Zal didn't, but he hoped it wouldn't be necessary. "Once Scrillia has spoken to him, you should spend some time with Dharl."

"I will. I loved being with my dad when I was younger, but my memories of him cooking and his pride in his claxx flowers doesn't sit naturally with him being a member of the Sentinel League."

Zal had explained his father's job, and it reminded him a little of MI6, but it was hard to put Dharl in the role of 007. "He's still your dad. His job doesn't change that."

"True, and there's some things I want to discuss with him, but while I wait, there's something else that's also important."

Devlin wasn't sure what Zal was alluding to. "What's that then?"

"I need to show you off."

He laughed and then realised Zal wasn't joking. "Zal, I'm not a trophy you've won."

"If I'm not out there showing my winnings, then some might think it was a one-off thing and you'll be up for playing with a new tail. And neither of us wants that."

While he knew Zal was only elaborating on the metaphor he didn't like being spoken about in such a manner. "I'm not your possession. I'm certainly not a prize that can be won or lost in a game."

Zal cocked his head to one side. Devlin had expected him to rush to apologise, not this slow consideration. "In Chroalian culture it is a bit like a prize. Don't you say similar things on Earth? Like to win someone's heart?"

"Yes, but it's gentle and romantic. Not a battle over who gets to fuck me."

"But that's what the ensigns want."

Devlin thought he was facing another cultural difference he might have to tread carefully around. "The point for me is that sort of language isn't for people who care about each other. It's about just having sex with them and nothing more, and that's not all you want, right?"

"Oh!" Zal's jaw dropped. "Not at all. I didn't mean it to come across like that."

He was going to have to be patient. "We both want everyone to know we're together, but could you think a little more about the language you use?"

"I will be more careful. I didn't think it would be that contentious." Zal stood and held out his hand. "Let me take you to the Bubble Bar, so we can sit in a viewport, not hidden away in one of the rooms. I want people to see me being happy in your company."

Devlin took his hand and let Zal pull him to his feet. "How about we have some of that wine you introduced me to?"

Zal's cheeks pinked. "When we get back. I'm not drinking that in public with you because it could be construed as I'm having to drug you in order to get you into my bed."

Devlin laughed and they left his cabin. He had some reservations about this, but if going out took Zal's mind off his father, then he was happy to go along. They fell into step and Devlin smiled as Zal wrapped his tail around Devlin's waist.

No one stared at them outright in the corridors or the elevator, but there were definite covert glances. He was glad Zal had not suggested the mess as he didn't think he'd want to be on full display just yet. It was one thing for their relationship to become known organically, another for his private life to be smeared like roadkill across a wet motorway.

They'd not visited the Bubble Bar since the evening he'd come aboard; there'd been too much going on and other things to see, but as they took seats in one of the viewports, it felt like the perfect backdrop. There were self-service pods on the far wall and Zal returned with two bright-blue drinks.

"This is a favourite of mine. I had it first on a space station around the orbit of Secrota 4 during a research trip to collect stardust from a meteorite storm which had an unusual pattern."

Devlin liked that Zal shared this sort of thing with him. "I daresay there might have been other memories associated with it, given some of the stories Brilli and Appla were telling."

"I know it sounded like I was wild and free, but I wasn't that bad. Other Chroalians were far more adventurous than me. This drink marked my first published paper. The data I gathered on Secrota 4 was unique." He leant forward. "A bit like you. So it's only fitting I share this drink with you."

"You're a smooth-talking sod."

"Sod? A clump of soil?"

Devlin laughed. "I don't think that translates well. Let's just say you have a lovely turn of phrase that will get you what you want from me."

Zal waved his tail. "What is it you think I want?"

"I don't think, *I know* you want a kiss. Maybe even more, but that'll have to wait until later and in private."

Zal shifted closer and Devlin welcomed Zal's hand on his jaw. "You know, I think humans are my favourite species."

"That's quite something."

"It is, as I've sampled a variety and none of them are as

delectable as you. And I think you're the very best of your species, so I must be a lucky soul."

They exchanged a soft kiss. Devlin wasn't averse to public displays of affection, but both he and Zal had influential roles on board and that warranted a little decorum. He pulled back to see Zal's eyes turning purple.

Devlin had no issue with Zal's more interesting past—he'd benefited from Zal's creative lovemaking skills, but he was not going to let the comment go without redress. "I'm rather taken with Chroalians as well. Although I've not dabbled with many other aliens, I think you'll hold my attention."

"How magnanimous of you. But at least it's a warning for me not to be complacent."

Devlin sat back and Zal pouted, but Devlin wanted to try the blue concoction. It was zingy, citrus-like, and not what he was expecting from the colour. A burst of refreshing flavour like nothing else, and it reminded him of Zal. "Oh, I could get used to those."

He noticed Zal's attention was elsewhere, and he saw he was distracted by the arrival of Brilli and Appla. Devlin found himself shunted to one side as Appla inserted themselves between them, grabbing Zal's hands. "Brilli told me what happened. I'm so sorry. I didn't know."

"It's okay. I understand it wasn't personal, Appla, and Brilli told me you weren't involved."

Devlin relinquished his seat—it was either that or get batted in the face by Appla's tail. Brilli took the space next to Zal on the other side of the viewport, and he suddenly felt surplus to requirements.

He scanned the area, looking for a spare seat he could borrow but instead saw several people staring in their direction, watching Zal sandwiched between his friends while Devlin stood on the periphery. This would not help the narrative that Zal was interested in him for more than a passing dalliance.

"Why don't I get drinks?" he offered, more for something to do than out of want. He headed over to the dispenser and tapped at the screen a couple of times, his flustered state not helping.

"What are you after?" Devlin turned to see a Chroalian a few years older than Zal wearing a lieutenant's uniform. He was attractive, with high cheekbones and bright-red hair.

"They're a blue drink—I'm not sure of the name."

"Texlas, maybe. Have a bit of zing to them."

"Sounds about right."

He held out his hand, and Devlin was surprised he was holding it in the human custom to shake hands rather than press their palms together. "I'm Gahild, a research engineer. We haven't been officially introduced, but I helped investigate your theory about the fake boarding."

The name was familiar, but it might have been from one of the reports that had been presented. He started to answer but Zal appeared at his side, Zal's tail wrapping itself possessively around Devlin's waist. "What are you doing over here?"

"Getting drinks for your friends."

Zal looked pensive. "They aren't staying. I told them they were interrupting, and we'd meet them for dinner another time."

Gahild grinned. "I've my own partner to be getting back to, but Ambassador Taylor looked like he needed help with the machine."

"Thank you, but looks like I'm good now," Devlin said.

Gahild excused himself and Zal's tail tightened around Devlin's waist and he bit his lip.

"Sorry, I didn't invite them."

"It's okay, let's go and finish our drinks," Devlin said.

Devlin was conscious they were being watched, but he was also glad that Zal had recognised his discomfort at the situation. He stroked Zal's cheek. "Or we can head back to your cabin? Have a couple of glasses of that special wine you mentioned."

Zal smiled. "A marvellous idea. I've something special I wanted to give you as well, but I was waiting for the right time."

Devlin wondered what that might be and they left the Bubble Bar. While he understood Zal's need to come out tonight, he was far happier to be on their own. "You know," he said as they entered the elevator, "this will be the first night on board where we can be together without me having to go back to my own cabin."

Zal chirruped, a noise he'd heard a couple of times when Zal was especially happy. "Oh, Devlin, let's hurry up. But you've a bigger bed. Let me grab a couple of things from my cabin, and I'll be right there."

Devlin entered his cabin and smiled. They'd been cautious

about spending the night together as the ship's computer would be able to track them, but since they were now no longer hiding, he was going to enjoy tonight. It wasn't even just the sex, but the idea of sleeping next to Zal and waking up with him, although Zal's Chroalian culture might be more interested in the sex, but that was a separate conversation.

Zal arrived clutching a bottle with his other hand behind his back. "Close your eyes; it's a surprise."

He did as he was told and held out his hand. He cracked open an eye and was delighted to find a packet of gingernut biscuits. "Oh, Zal, wherever did you get these?"

"I may have smuggled aboard a small stash of Earth delicacies."

He loved that Zal had been so thoughtful. "Thank you. I'll savour every single one."

"I can set up a stasis chamber so they last longer."

"No one wants soggy gingernuts."

Zal wrinkled his nose. "Is that meant to be a euphemism?"

Devlin carefully placed the biscuits and the wine on the side and pulled Zal into his arms, walking backwards towards the bed, determined to show Zal how pleased he was with his gift. "Let's just say you deserve a large reward for your thoughtfulness."

Zal let out a soft *ouff* as they toppled backwards and Devlin was flipped onto his back. "I'm not one for boasting about my achievement, but I am rather pleased with the biscuits."

Devlin surrendered to the kiss. Zal was a wonderful kisser

and Devlin loved to be pinned underneath him. "I understand that you're also very good at removing clothing."

"An expert. Especially if it means I can get my hands on a certain ambassador's fuzzy bits."

Devlin laughed and Zal sat back, stripping away his clothes, Devlin quick to follow, and once he was naked Zal pounced, knocking him back and demanding another kiss. He moaned as Zal's tail stroked his side. "You've a very clever tail."

He'd not brought up trying new things in bed, but now they didn't have to rush their lovemaking, he wanted to remind Zal that he'd be up for experimenting.

"I really want to show you some of the things we can do with it, but the shape means I think we'll have to work up to it." Zal sat up so he was kneeling between Devlin's thigh, the tip of his arrow-head-shaped tail circling Devlin's belly button. "Tonight I really want to fuck you, but next time I'm gonna work you open with my fingers, make sure you're super ready and then plug you with my tail. Then I'm gonna ride you. Your cock buried in me while you're filled by my tail."

"Oh, fuck, Zal. I'm so hard even thinking about it."

"Me too, Devlin. But I won't rush this. Your anatomy's different to mine, and I want to enjoy seeing you come apart. Tonight I want to bury my cock in you, not my tail."

Devlin was so hard and desperate that he'd have let Zal do whatever he wanted. Zal grabbed the lube, and Devlin couldn't take his eyes off Zal's tail as it slid lower and Zal wrapped the long blue appendage around Devlin's cock, the scales bristling as they slid over his hard shaft. He gasped as Zal's fingers worked him open. He'd never felt as wanted as he did when he was with Zal as if he was someone worthy to be worshipped and his pleasure wasn't an afterthought.

"You're so gorgeous, Devlin."

Zal removed his fingers, and he felt the loss keenly until Zal replaced them with his cock, filling him, claiming him. Devlin's head spun as Zal fucked him while his clever tail continued to bring him pleasure. He would be ruined for other men—no one could replace Zal.

The pace was borderline brutal, and Devlin loved it. Zal knew what he needed, every thrust pushing Devlin closer to the edge, and he gave in to the building maelstrom of his desire, his orgasm crashing over him as he came. Zal sped up, chasing his own release and came with a shout, calling out Devlin's name.

He had vague recollections of Zal withdrawing and conducting a perfunctory clean-up before being gathered into his arms.

Devlin sighed in contentment as he rested his head on Zal's chest. "I must say my first couple of weeks on board have lived up to the drama I expected, although I didn't think I'd be at the centre of a staged event."

Zal carded his fingers through Devlin's hair. It was nice, soothing even. "I can't see it getting any calmer from here on in."

"If I wanted calm I'd have stayed at home, and I'm right where I want to be."

Chapter Twenty-Five

Zal had been proud of the biscuits. Gingernuts might be an odd name for them, but they seemed to be Devlin's favourites, and he had several other things in his stash that he planned to give to Devlin every so often to either help with the inevitable homesickness or for special occasions. But there was something he wanted to do to cement their relationship, and that meant he would need to speak to his father, and he couldn't avoid the conversation about finding out he was a member of the Sentinel League. On reflection, he should have realised that his dad wasn't just tagging along with his mum, and it grated on him that he was meant to be a decent scientist with good observational skills, yet he'd completely overlooked this.

Zal had left Devlin in his cabin, using the excuse he was needed in his lab for a little while, but instead, he made his way to a different deck. Devlin was working through a language exercise and the reading he'd been given, trying to build himself a pattern of daily life when on board the *Endeavour,* which Zal had thought an admirable idea.

"Hello," he called as he entered his parents' rooms. He'd checked that his mother was busy but that she'd spoken to Dharl about Zal's recent revelation, as he wanted to talk to his dad without her brand of helping, which he was usually all for but wasn't what he needed today.

Dharl emerged from the bedroom into the sitting area part of the family and double occupancy rooms. "Ah, Zal. I was expecting you to turn up sooner rather than later."

"Yeah, well, it's not every day you realise you've missed your father being a strategic military mastermind."

Dharl laughed. "I'm not sure I'd refer to myself quite in those terms, but I was surprised you had no inkling of my profession."

"I'm not feeling overly impressed with my powers of deduction. But you could have said something."

Dharl sat down and patted the space next to him on the sofa. "You know your mother isn't allowed to discuss the intricacies of much of her work and, as most of what I do dovetails with hers, I'm in a similar position."

"But at least I knew she was an ambassador. I thought you were just there so you wouldn't have to be apart."

He smiled. "It's certainly a positive side to my position. I was her bodyguard originally, so my role expanded."

"Bodyguard? That wasn't the story you told us."

"It's only a slight difference. I was rostered to protect her, and one evening when she was engaged in a different way of making alliances, she made a quick exit, and I found her, still partially clothed and looking for the best way to sneak away without being caught."

Zal suspected there was more to the story. "But you said she had to win your trust."

"Yes, I was already in love with her, and it wasn't easy to have watched her from afar, taking lovers that weren't me, and when the incident happened, I finally found the nerve to talk to her."

He would have hated being in the same position, and even the thought of standing by while Devlin romanced other people turned his stomach. "I don't understand how you could have coped with that."

"I was a nobody, a guard, and although I was in training for the Sentinel League, I wasn't the sort of person your mother would have noticed. Maybe that's unfair. I wasn't on her list of people she would need to be cordial with, but she said she'd seen me looking at her."

"I... but..."

"Zal, I love your mum very much. I always have, and once we were dating, we had to be careful. Much like you and Devlin, it wasn't the right time for everyone to know. She didn't take other lovers but had to act as if she did, and for the first few cycles together it was difficult. Once I passed my entrance into the Sentinel

League, I was deemed a suitable candidate by your mother's parents."

He couldn't imagine his parents applying a similar rule to him, only giving their blessing if a potential partner were the right calibre. "I never thought Moma and Ipa were like that."

"Your grandparents are wonderful people, and they wanted the best for their only daughter. Things were different then, especially in the circles your mum grew up in. It made us conscious of what we wouldn't do to our own children."

"You didn't need to be so secretive over your Sentinel League involvement though."

"I didn't think I was." He smiled. "I checked with your brother and sister after your mum said you were surprised, and they assured me they both knew."

Zal huffed. "I can't believe I was that dense."

"Don't be so hard on yourself, Zal. You left home to study and while we saw you regularly, you weren't living as close to us as your siblings were. Your research took you away travelling, so why would you have been looking for it? If on anyone, the fault lies with me."

Put like that, there wasn't any blame to assign. His father had done a job that protected his mum, and he couldn't be annoyed by that. However, it wasn't his sole grievance. "I guess so. But you were hiding your involvement with testing Devlin."

"Yes, but then I couldn't have said anything, and from what I saw, I was confident the testing was a formality more than anything else. He made—makes—you so happy I had to think he was the right sort of man to be an ambassador and my boy's partner. But I also had my orders."

"Would you have said something if Devlin had given you cause for concern?"

"I'd have found a way." He slapped Zal's thigh. "But he is a wonderful young man. I couldn't be happier that you not only found each other but were able to be together."

"I'm glad you approve because there is something I wanted to talk to you about, as well as you being a super-secret spy."

"Anything wrong?" Dharl asked.

"Not wrong. I wanted to get your advice."

Dharl rested his tail on Zal's shoulder. "That sounds serious. Come on, let's see if we can smooth you out a bit."

"I'm not a wrinkle that needs ironing," he said with a chuckle as he sat. "But I do need to speak to someone, and I think you might have gone through this with Mum. Or something similar."

Dharl tilted his head to one side, his earrings jangling. "Now you have piqued my interest. What's this about?"

"Devlin." He didn't want to sound like a whining idiot but this was getting stupid, especially after last night and Brilli and Appla forgetting their boundaries and interrupting their date that had meant to be him showing off his new relationship with the sexiest biped on the ship. "He's an obvious attraction for many of the crew, the captain included, and I felt really jealous over Holjin even though I had no reason to."

"You've never felt this deeply for anyone, Zal. You're showing natural tendencies but you need to be careful not to go too far. Jealousy is not pleasant for the one experiencing it or the one it's directed at."

Zal adored Devlin, loved him like no other, and he knew Devlin loved him back. "I know, and likewise Devlin is adapting to how close I am to Brilli and Appla."

"We are an affectionate species, and they are close friends of yours. I'm sure he is trying his best."

"He is. He was also surprised I was so jealous over Holjin but no one else in the crew. But now I am a bit worried in case I do end up getting jealous over someone else." He sighed. "Given Mum's role, maybe you have had to deal with similar emotions and could help advise me how not to overreact if it was to happen?"

"Ah, I see." He squeezed Zal's knee. "Your mum has the sort of job where she is constantly meeting new people and has to be warm and welcoming, and if I didn't completely trust her we'd have separated years ago. But although you love him, you haven't known Devlin for long, and trust does need to be earned."

"He's not done anything that would lead me not to trust him." Devlin was attentive and loving, and he'd not been interested in anyone else in the crew apart from friendship. "Especially if you compare his actions to what I was like from when I first left Chroalia."

"Well, you were a little wild but no worse than most students. You know the real story now of how I started dating your mother."

He'd heard versions of the story countless times, the more risqué details had been added as he'd got older, and the part of Dharl being her bodyguard was new. "But you didn't mind and could see she was capable of loving only you."

"Yes, but what's the issue here? You're judging Devlin on what you used to do, not his actions. Do you believe Devlin is bothered by your past flings and he thinks you'll be interested in being with others?"

He wasn't sure; his emotions weren't easy to pin down. "He knows I was a little wild but also that I'm not into sharing with anyone when I'm in a committed relationship."

"We had to earn each other's trust. If me and your mum hadn't trusted each other, we wouldn't have stayed together during the times when people didn't know about our relationship. Your mum is a stunningly beautiful woman, always has been, and I am honoured that she consented to be my bond-mate. As we got older and she continued her diplomatic career, she once again started to attract people, but I've never doubted her, and there's been many times when she was offered a more physical way to build diplomatic ties..."

He did trust Devlin, but he knew Devlin might struggle with some of the Chroalian customs. "I think I'm overcompensating. Devlin isn't used to how Chroalians are more physical with their friends. And the connection I have with Brilli and Appla is a close one. I want him to trust me, and I want the others on board to know Devlin is mine and not a passing fling."

Dharl smiled knowingly. "I think you may already have had thoughts on how to do that. But what I can tell you, if I am right about where you are going with this, is once I was deemed worthy, me and your mum courted properly, full-on, nothing spared."

He knew that had gone on. Courtship was an ancient Chroalian tradition, still widely practised, a knowledge passed from parent to child. "I want to do the same for Devlin. I want to show him our customs, demonstrate that I appreciate that he left his planet so we could be together."

"We have many rituals, some of which are not to be undertaken lightly. Tell me, you are not one to be so easily riled, where's the jealousy coming from? An individual or situations? Or is it just Devlin's reaction to Brilli and Appla?"

"It's Holjin. He made no secret of what he'd like to do to Devlin. Although now he says it was an act because he knew Devlin was attached."

"The captain makes a pass at everyone—he even gave me the eye until he realised I was your mum's husband."

"What?" Zal was appalled, especially given his and Holjin's history.

"We met at a fancy reception before I was formally introduced, but once he knew I was attached, and to whom, he fell back to friendly without the flirting. But the point is, you know what Holjin's like—personally—and it's not him who has to keep your trust, it's Devlin."

"You're right. Devlin knows that and he said he hasn't any

issue with my past." Although Zal had recognised some apprehension about his continued close friendship with Brilli and Appla. "He's done nothing to encourage anyone."

"What's the issue, then?"

"I guess what it boils down to is I want everyone to know he's mine, and mine for keeps." He wasn't jealous of others on the ship; this was about wanting to show Devlin how important he was to him, at the same time as showing everyone else. "We've begun our public relationship, but I know already it's not going to be enough."

"In what way? It strikes me your relationship being seen as organically evolving would be the most sensible approach in your situation."

Zal didn't want a slow build, he needed more and quick. "Because it will appear to be just the start, no one will know he's been mine for a while and might even think he's still available."

"That would still be the case whatever you do. For some Chroalians, a person is only unavailable once they have been courted and handfasted." Dharl stared at him. "Oh, Zal, you want it all already?"

"I have for a while. You know I gave him my earring when I left Earth, and he's since given it back, and I don't like it."

"That he gave it back? You can't judge him for that. He wouldn't have known our customs."

He didn't know how to explain this—it wasn't as clear-cut as that. "Devlin didn't know the significance when I gave it to him, but I explained once he came aboard, and then he gave it back, thinking I wasn't ready for him to have it." He stroked the offending piece of jewellery that sat on his left ear. "But now I know I want him to have it with everything that entails. And even if he couldn't have worn it, it gave me great peace when we weren't together to know he had it. This must sound stupid."

"Not at all. The attachment is to the time you spent apart; your earring being in Devlin's possession meant that he would still have a piece of you with him." Dharl placed his arm around Zal's shoulders. "You're a sensitive and empathetic man, Zal. Your feelings are an important part of what makes you who you are."

He was glad his dad could understand. "Then will you support me through the courtship? I intend to start in earnest as soon as possible."

"I sense I won't be able to persuade you to wait a little longer; this is a big step to take." Dharl raised an eyebrow. "Some couples wait decades, and it's not to be rushed."

He thought his dad might say something about taking his time. "I can't wait. I need to do this. In part, I want to show my commitment to Devlin after he left Earth so we could be together."

"You don't have to undergo the courtship to cohabit and show you're committed to each other."

"It's not that. It's knowing deep down that he's it for me, so why wait when I can begin this now and end it with Devlin as my recognised bond-mate? Bonded and together."

He yelped as Dharl unexpectedly pulled him into a tight hug.

"Oh, Zal, I couldn't be more pleased. I had to make sure you were ready, but I can see that you are. I must admit, me and your mother did wonder if you'd be one of the lifelong flitters."

Zal hadn't realised they thought that about him. "Really?"

"Not that there'd be anything wrong with it if you had turned out to want to stay unattached, but it can be lonely at times."

"I'd always thought I'd find someone. I wouldn't have wanted it when I was younger, but I knew I wanted a permanent companion at some point. Now I know who my special person is and I get to have them as we travel the universe."

He'd thought Telgan might be the one, but that idea hadn't lasted long, and they'd muddled on well enough, but in reality, it had only made Zal realise towards the end what it was he was missing. Meeting Devlin on Earth had been a wonderful, unexpected bonus that had been meant as a holiday fling and ended up being so much more.

"I dated Telgan for ages," Zal said.

"But we all knew he wasn't someone you would want to permanently tie your tail to."

It was as if Dharl had read his mind. "I wish you would have told me."

"You wouldn't have listened. Part of the job of being a parent is knowing where to interfere and when to leave alone. You were happy enough, not the universe's most exciting of relationships, and I can't pretend we were upset when you split up."

His parents, his mum in particular, had made comments but

had never been hostile to his ex, and it didn't matter now. "It's ancient history. Now I need your guidance on my future with Devlin."

"As I told your brother as he courted Asdin, it's only as complicated as you want to make it. There are only six things that need to be done, and they can be executed simply or as contrived as you like. Just because something is simple doesn't mean it doesn't require effort, and it is the effort that is important, not the grandiosity of the act."

Dharl stood and then left the room, only to return with a notebook and pen. It wasn't usual for them to use paper. The notebook had an elaborate cover, an iridescent blue with the outlines of gold hexagons. "What have you there?"

"I picked this up on Earth. I liked it and thought I might try and do some calligraphy, but for some reason I couldn't bring myself to use it. And now I know why." He held it out for Zal to take, which he did. "You should use this to chart your journey with Devlin."

He ran his hand over the surface. "It's lovely. I'm not used to writing with an actual pen."

"There are plenty of practice apps you can use. Don't find an excuse when a solution is easier. This is a piece of Earth, a link for Devlin back to his home planet."

The symbolism wasn't lost on Zal. "Oh, yes, I see. We could both record our thoughts in it. Something unique for us."

Dharl grinned. "We all need to feel special. You and Devlin

have a wonderful story to tell about how you got together, and now you can capture your continued journey."

"I just need to know what it is I need to do." He'd heard courtships were very personal and reflected the couple involved, which given he hadn't known Devlin all that long made things a little tricky.

"The first step is declaring your intent to Devlin. You'll need to explain it to him, and it might take some doing since it's not his culture." From the side of the chair they were sitting on, he dug out his tablet. "Then you can consider the six steps to harmony."

He'd been thinking about how to broach the idea with Devlin, and he had decided on a private moment in his cabin, trying not to trip over his words. But before he did that, he wanted to know what the path was.

Dharl handed Zal the device and he saw the list.

Courtship: Six Steps on the Road to Harmony
1. *Show devotion without stating the words*
2. *Use new words to profess old things*
3. *A gift like no other*
4. *Physical bond*
5. *Beyond the mundane*
6. *Accepting the forever, and a day*

Zal knew the titles of the steps already; every Chroalian was taught them, and seeing them wasn't very helpful. He was hoping for more direction rather than these vagaries he could get any-where. "But what do they mean?"

"I can't tell you that—each one will mean something different to everyone. A triad or quad will have a dynamic that doesn't match yours and Devlin's. If you are truly ready, then go and re-flect on these, and then work with Devlin to devise an action to meet each one. Don't overthink it."

He should have expected this. Chroalian customs were often traditions that had multiple ways of being celebrated. Every family had their own ritual for pretty much every holiday, so it stood to reason this would be no different. He decided to try a different tack. "What did you and Mum do?"

"Me and your mum aren't you and Devlin, so there'd be no point copying what we did," Dharl replied with a wry smile. "I will send you the list. Go and spend some time in a contemplation bub-ble or meditate on it."

"I thought a parent was meant to give guidance."

"I will, but I will not do your thinking for you. Once you have some thoughts, we can discuss how you can implement them."

He might be frustrated by his dad's response, but he couldn't argue. "I suppose."

"Go and confirm Devlin wants to take these steps with you. You're assuming he does, but humans may have their own cus-toms and you should be conscious about working those into any-thing you do."

Dharl was right, not just about Devlin, but the courtship was theirs to own, and it was why it was such a personal journey and meant so much. If everyone did the same, there would be nothing special for each couple. He gave his dad a final hug and returned to his cabin. Over the years, he'd tackled all sorts of complicated problems and conducted research on previously unexplained phenomena, so this should not be an issue. But as he lay on his bed, his mind was a complete blank. Maybe this was because he was trying to take the first step of the journey on his own when he should already be going hand in hand with Devlin.

Chapter Twenty-Six

Devlin was pleased with the progress he was making with his Chroalian. Theirs was an interesting language, reminding him of a mix of Russian and Latin with a sprinkling of Japanese, and once he'd got his head around the alphabet, it was as if something clicked. He was looking forward to surprising Zal with his linguistic capabilities in a couple of weeks—once he'd built enough vocabulary to move beyond fruits and vegetables and asking directions to a swimming pool.

The communication panel pinged. "Incoming message from Lieutenant Catenmir."

"Accept. Zal, aren't you on duty?"

"Just finished. Can you come to my cabin? I've something I'd like to share with you."

"More biscuits?"

Zal laughed. "Better than biscuits."

"I'm not sure that's possible, Zal. I hope you're not setting yourself up for a fall over my expectations."

"Just come here."

Devlin sensed an edge of nervousness in Zal's tone and decided now was not the time to push the biscuit narrative. "I'll be right over."

Zal had spent the last couple of days in a contemplative mood, not pensive, but distracted over something. He'd not sensed that Zal was less interested in him in any way, but he was brooding over something, and if Devlin was to try to pin it down, he'd say it might be to do with both the discovery of his father's more active role in the Chroalian security services than he'd known and the story of how his parents had met having more layers and flavour than he'd been told before.

He'd get to the bottom of it one way or another, although he'd let Zal keep his thoughts to himself a little longer before he stepped in, and he wouldn't let the worry fester as these things had a habit of causing more damage if left unresolved. For tonight, he had a surefire way of distracting Zal. Even if it didn't entail biscuits.

As he entered Zal's cabin, he was surprised to see the lights dimmed and a series of electric candles had been placed in and around the seating area and in front of the porthole, and it was positively romantic. Zal sat on a mound of cushions dressed in one of his evening robes, usually reserved for dances and galas. "Well, this is special."

Zal patted the cushions next to him. "Sit next to me. I wanted to talk to you about something very important, and it's taken me a while to figure out how I wanted to say it."

Given the effort Zal had gone to, this was not going to be a bad thing, and Devlin quickly sat down as close as he could, intrigued with what Zal wanted to talk about. "I'm always willing to listen."

"It's about a Chroalian tradition, and I've been researching human customs and haven't come across anything that similar."

"I'm all for experiencing new things, and I'm sure you'd not ask me to do something you think I'd object to."

"Not object but maybe I think I was pushing things too soon." Zal held out his hand, and he saw the earring Devlin had returned. "I want you to have this. I am ready for you to have this."

Devlin picked it up. He was so happy to have it back, and had regretted returning it to begin with. "Are you proposing we get married?"

"I suppose that's the closest to what humans do, but it's a much more protracted engagement, and the couple undertakes the journey to harmony together. Different symbolic steps between agreeing to start the journey and us undertaking our life-binding ceremony."

Zal sounded so unsure, as if Devlin might say no. But that was the farthest from Devlin's mind.

"Sounds all kinds of wonderful to me. Zal, I love you, and

can't think of anything better than working together in whatever way you need from me."

Zal leant in and Devlin brushed his lips to Zal's, not deepening the kiss as otherwise he'd not be able to stop himself knocking Zal backwards onto the cushions, and he suspected there was much more Zal wanted to discuss.

"Oh, Devlin. You make me so happy. The custom involves six steps that a couple or partners negotiate. They've got ridiculously vague titles but that means we can interpret what it means to us and our thoughts and what we want from our relationship."

Zal looked so alive as he spoke, and Devlin couldn't imagine anyone saying no to such an idea. "It's a wonderful concept, Zal. It sounds like a metaphor for a long life committed to each other. Having to decide what works and making sure we're both comfortable with what we do is the way I'd like to think our life together would be like."

Zal produced a notebook from under the cushion he was sitting on. Devlin hadn't seen any paper on board the ship so he was intrigued as to why Zal had it. "My father picked this up when we were on Earth. He gave it to me to record our courtship, thinking it would be a nice link back to your home."

Devlin took the book. It looked the type to have come from a museum gift shop or craft market with a shiny multi-blue toned cover with gold marking, making Devlin think of the patterns of Zal's scales. "It's perfect. We can write thoughts and decisions and then keep it as a memento, although depending on the content we may not wish to let anyone else read it."

"I'll explain the six steps but they are all a matter of individual interpretation. The first one is to show devotion without stating the words—that could have all sorts of meanings."

Devlin grinned. "I can think of one almost immediately if they are allowed to have a physical nature to them."

Zal's eyes widened and his irises began to turn purple. "I do love the way your mind works."

"If they are all like that, we might be through the whole thing in a week."

Zal nuzzled his nose. "As much as I love the idea of it being a long fuck fest, and one of the steps is called a physical bond, I do think we should try to have non-orgasmic aspects to the others as well. Just to make sure we're covered."

"That's just you being greedy."

"You know I want everything when it comes to you."

"Is there an external arbitrator who confirms we have completed the ritual so we'll be pledged to each other for the rest of our lives?" he asked.

"Not exactly, we have to fill in the paperwork for our bonding, but no one checks we've done our homework. If they weren't bothered, there are other legal ways of confirming a partnership."

Devlin was still holding the earring, and he held it up to his ear. "I'm not sure it'll suit me. What do you reckon?"

Zal took it and laid it across his hand. "We could have it made into something you could wear around your wrist."

Devlin liked the idea of wearing the gift like a bracelet as dangly earrings weren't his usual style, but he thought there was something missing. "I don't have an earring to give you though. Aren't you meant to receive one from me?"

"I'd like to hold the official ceremony on Chroalia, so you could have a set of earrings made there." Zal bit his lip, and Devlin was glad he'd brought it up because he was sure this had been in Zal's thoughts. "If you want to."

"Absolutely. I'll spend some time on a design, I'd love for whatever I give you to represent my feelings. Traditionally we exchange wedding bands, would you consider wearing a ring?"

Zal looked down at his hand and wriggled his fingers. "I'd have to be careful of the metal because of the lab, but I'd have no issue in upholding your customs. Do you have a set?"

"No, usually they are made or selected by the couple. Occasionally, they get handed down but not in my family." His dad had been buried with his, and he had no idea what had become of his mum's.

Zal tapped the notebook. "We should put our designs in here."

"Good idea."

"Devlin, I need you to know that I've never wanted this with anyone else. I know I've had other partners, some more long-term than others, but nothing I've felt before comes close to what I feel for you."

Devlin knew that, but it meant so much to hear the words.

"Zal, it's the same for me."

"There will be people who look at us and think we're going far too quickly—many Chroalians take years to get to this stage—but I thought I'd lost you once and I'm not going to wait around because someone thinks we're doing it wrong. I love you. I want everyone to know you've consented to make me the happiest person in the universe."

They might have a lot more to discuss but Zal couldn't say things like that and not have Devlin react. He pushed Zal back onto the cushions. "You're mine, Zal. I'm yours, and I won't let anything drive us apart."

"We have a lifetime to explore the universe, and I can't wait to see where it takes us next."

Devlin kissed him. There was so much ahead of him that no other human would get to experience, but the reason it would be wonderful was because he would get to see it all with Zal.

Acknowledgements

Endless thanks to Lou and Toshi for the ever helpful feedback.

About the Author

Rebecca Cohen spends her days dreaming of living in a Tudor manor house, or a Georgian mansion. Alas, the closest she comes to this is through her characters in her historical romance novels. She also dreams of intergalactic adventures and fantasy realms, but because she's not yet got her space or dimensional travel plans finalised, she lives happily in leafy Hertfordshire, England, with her husband and young son. She can often be found with a pen in one hand and sloe gin with lemon tonic in the other.

Facebook
www.facebook.com/rebecca.cohen.710

Facebook Group
www.facebook.com/groups/498970581304907

Website
www.rebeccacohenwrites.wordpress.com

Instagram
@rebeccacohenwriter

Newsletter Signup
dl.bookfunnel.com/g6xh4q8a8v

Other NineStar books by this author

Devlin Taylor, Earth Ambassador Series

Ministry of Alien Relations

CONNECT WITH NINESTAR PRESS

WEBSITE: NINESTARPRESS.COM

FACEBOOK: NINESTARPRESS

X: @NINESTARPRESS

INSTAGRAM: NINESTARPRESS

BLUESKY: NINESTARPRESS

THREADS: @NINESTARPRESS